YORK NOTES

JANE EYRE

CHARLOTTE BRONTË

WORKBOOK BY CAROLINE WOOLFE

D0336028

PEARSON

YORK
PRESS

The right of Caroline Woolfe to be identified as the Author of this Work
has been asserted by her in accordance with the Copyright, Designs and
Patents Act 1988

YORK PRESS
322 Old Brompton Road, London SW5 9JH

PEARSON EDUCATION LIMITED
Edinburgh Gate, Harlow,
Essex CM20 2JE, United Kingdom

Associated companies, branches and representatives throughout the world

First published 2016

10 9 8 7 6 5 4 3 2 1

ISBN 978–1–2921–3811–4

Illustrations by Jérôme Brasseur; and Alan Batley (page 62 only)
Phototypeset by DTP Media
Printed in Slovakia

Photo credits: © iStock/AVTG for page 9 top / meirion matthias/Shutterstock/Peter Coleman for page
15 top / Lisovskay a Natalia/Shutterstock for page 17 top / Konstanttin/Shutterstock for page 19 top /
Brenda Linskey/Shutterstock for page 21 top / Serg64/Shutterstock for page 29 top / Alexandra Lande/
Shutterstock for page 33 top / © iStock/Danielrao for page 41 top / LanKS/Shutterstock for page 57
bottom / Victor Kilygin/Shutterstock for page 65 bottom / Kevin Tracey/Shutterstock for page 67 top
/ Vova Shevch uk/Shutterstock for page 68 bottom 1 / Medioimages/Thinkstock for page 68 bottom
2 / Ispace/Shutterstock for page 69 bottom 1 / Rudchenk o Liliia/Shutterstock for page 69 bottom 2 /
Purestock/Thinkstock for page 70 top

CONTENTS

PART FOUR:
THEMES, CONTEXTS AND SETTINGS

PART FIVE:
FORM, STRUCTURE AND LANGUAGE

PART SIX:
PROGRESS BOOSTER

PART ONE: GETTING STARTED

Preparing for assessment

HOW WILL I BE ASSESSED ON MY WORK ON *JANE EYRE*?

All exam boards are different but whichever course you are following, your work will be examined through these three Assessment Objectives:

Assessment Objectives	Wording	Worth thinking about ...
AO1	Read, understand and respond to texts. Students should be able to: ● maintain a critical style and develop an informed personal response ● use textual references, including quotations, to support and illustrate interpretations.	● How well do I know what happens, what people say, do, etc? ● What do I think about the key ideas in the novel? ● How can I support my viewpoint in a really convincing way? ● What are the best quotations to use and when should I use them?
AO2	Analyse the language, form and structure used by a writer to create meanings and effects, using relevant subject terminology where appropriate.	● What specific things does the writer 'do'? What choices has Charlotte Brontë made? (Why this particular word, phrase or paragraph here? Why does this event happen at this point?) ● What effects do these choices create? Anticipation? Sense of threat? Reflective mood?
AO3	Show understanding of the relationships between texts and the contexts in which they were written.	● What can I learn about society from the book? (What does it tell me about the power held by different types of people in Charlotte Brontë's day, for example?) ● What was society like in Charlotte Brontë's time? Can I see it reflected in the text?

If you are studying OCR then you will also have a small number of marks allocated to AO4:

AO4	Use a range of vocabulary and sentence structures for clarity, purpose and effect, with accurate spelling and punctuation.	● How accurately and clearly do I write? ● Are there small errors of grammar, spelling and punctuation I can get rid of?

Look out for the Assessment Objective labels throughout your York Notes Workbook – these will help to focus your study and revision!

The text used in this Workbook is the Penguin Classics edition, 2006.

How to use your York Notes Workbook

There are lots of ways your Workbook can support your study and revision of *Jane Eyre*. There is no 'right' way – choose the one that suits your learning style best.

1) Alongside the York Notes Study Guide and the text	2) As a 'stand-alone' revision programme	3) As a form of mock-exam
Do you have the York Notes Study Guide for *Jane Eyre*?	Think you know *Jane Eyre* well?	Prefer to do all your revision in one go?
The contents of your Workbook are designed to match the sections in the Study Guide, so with the novel to hand you could:	Why not work through the Workbook systematically, either as you finish chapters, or as you study or revise certain aspects in class or at home.	You could put aside a day or two and work through the Workbook, page by page. Once you have finished, check all your answers in one go!
• read the relevant section(s) of the Study Guide and any part of the novel referred to; • complete the tasks in the same section in your Workbook.	You could make a revision diary and allocate particular sections of the Workbook to a day or week.	This will be quite a challenge, but it may be the approach you prefer.

HOW WILL THE WORKBOOK HELP YOU TEST AND CHECK YOUR KNOWLEDGE AND SKILLS?

Parts Two to **Five** offer a range of tasks and activities:

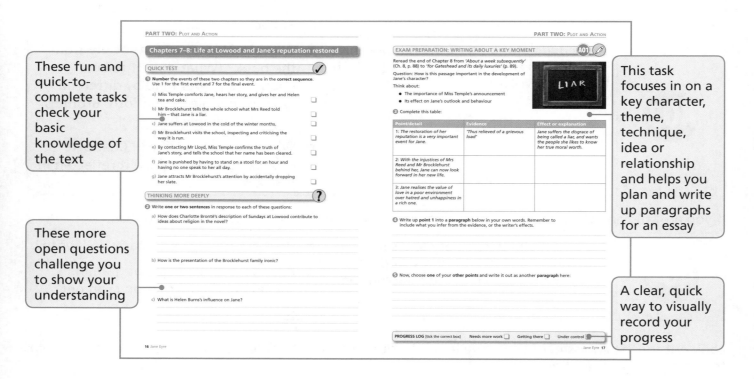

These fun and quick-to-complete tasks check your basic knowledge of the text

These more open questions challenge you to show your understanding

This task focuses in on a key character, theme, technique, idea or relationship and helps you plan and write up paragraphs for an essay

A clear, quick way to visually record your progress

Each Part ends with a **Practice task** to extend your revision:

An exam-style task for you to practise a full essay

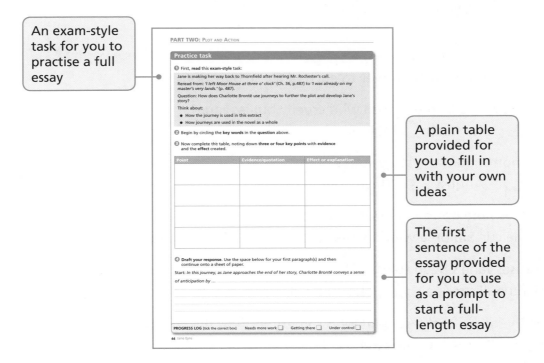

A plain table provided for you to fill in with your own ideas

The first sentence of the essay provided for you to use as a prompt to start a full-length essay

Part Six: Progress Booster helps you test your own key writing skills:

A sample of a student's writing challenges you to judge its strengths and weaknesses

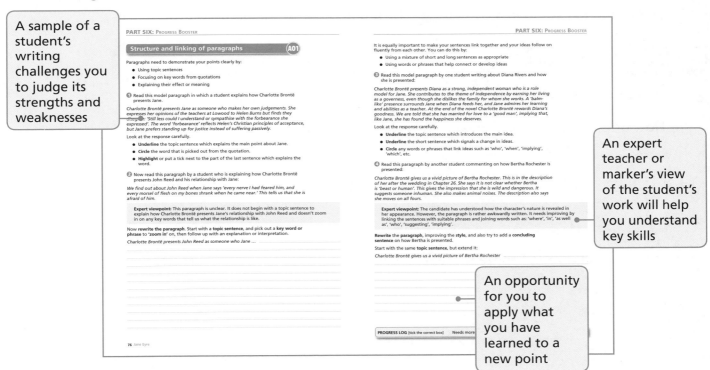

An expert teacher or marker's view of the student's work will help you understand key skills

An opportunity for you to apply what you have learned to a new point

Don't forget – these are just some examples of the Workbook contents. Inside there is much more to help you revise. For example:

- lots of samples of students' own work at different levels
- help with writing skills
- advice and tasks on writing about context
- a full answer key so you can check your answers
- a full-length practice exam task with guidance on what to focus on.

PART TWO: Plot and Action

Chapter 1: The young Jane is isolated and alone

QUICK TEST ✔

1 **Tick** the box for the correct answer to each of these questions:

a) What is the name of the person who cruelly bullies Jane?
Bessie ☐   John Reed ☐   Eliza Reed ☐

b) In what month does the story start?
January ☐   August ☐   November ☐

c) Where does Jane go to hide from everyone?
behind the curtain on a window seat ☐   under the dining table ☐   in the library ☐

d) What causes Jane's head to bleed?
Georgiana pulls her hair ☐   She cuts it on a bookshelf ☐   John throws a book at her ☐

e) What is the name of the servant who sometimes tells the children stories?
Abbot ☐   Bessie ☐   Mrs Reed ☐

f) How does Mrs Reed punish Jane for her outburst?   by locking her in the red-room ☐
by making her stand in a corner ☐   by sending her to the breakfast room ☐

THINKING MORE DEEPLY ?

2 Write **one** or **two sentences** in response to each of these questions:

a) How does the book that Jane reads help to create atmosphere?

b) How does Charlotte Brontë present John Reed as an unattractive character?

c) How does Charlotte Brontë use first person narrative to affect how the reader responds to Jane?

EXAM PREPARATION: WRITING ABOUT THE OPENING OF THE NOVEL A02

Reread the opening three paragraphs of Chapter 1 from *'There was no possibility'* to *'happy little children'* (p. 9).

Question: How does Charlotte Brontë use the opening of the novel to convey an impression of Jane's character and situation?

Think about:

- Jane's description of the weather and setting
- The contrasts between Jane and members of the Reed family

❸ Complete this table:

Point/detail	Evidence	Effect or explanation
1: *The description of a miserably cold day creates a dismal picture of Jane's experience.*	*'dreadful to me was the coming home in the raw twilight, with nipped fingers and toes'*	*Her physical suffering seems to reflect the emotional coldness she experiences.*
2: *Jane feels like an outsider with the Reed children.*		
3: *The Reeds enjoy comfort and luxury while Jane is excluded.*		

❹ Write up **point 1** into a **paragraph** below in your own words. Remember to include what you infer from the evidence, or the writer's effects.

....

....

....

....

....

❺ Now, choose **one** of your **other points** and write it out as another **paragraph** here:

....

....

....

....

....

....

....

PROGRESS LOG [tick the correct box]   Needs more work ☐   Getting there ☐   Under control ☐

Chapters 2–3: The red-room and its aftermath

QUICK TEST ✔

1 **Number** the events of these two chapters so they are in the **correct sequence**. Use 1 for the first event and 7 for the final event.

a) When it goes dark, Jane is frightened by a moving light, which she thinks could be a ghost. ☐

b) Jane awakes in her own bed to find Mr Lloyd, a kind apothecary, watching over her. ☐

c) Bessie and Miss Abbot force Jane into the red-room. ☐

d) Jane's screams bring the servants and Mrs Reed running to her. ☐

e) Jane looks around the room remembering that this is where her uncle died. ☐

f) Mr Lloyd questions Jane about her own family and her life with the Reeds at Gateshead. ☐

g) Jane falls unconscious when Mrs Reed again locks her in the red-room. ☐

THINKING MORE DEEPLY ?

2 Write **one** or **two sentences** in response to each of these questions:

a) What are Jane's feelings about going to school?

....
....
....
....

b) What do we learn about Jane's family history?

....
....
....
....

c) How does Charlotte Brontë present Bessie as the most sympathetic character at Gateshead?

....
....
....
....
....

EXAM PREPARATION: WRITING ABOUT HOW BRONTË CREATES TENSION (A02)

Reread Jane's description of her fear of a ghost from *'A singular notion dawned upon me.'* (Ch. 2, p. 20) to *'Bessie and Abbot entered.'* (p. 21).

Question: How does Charlotte Brontë build tension through this account of Jane's fearful thoughts?

Think about:

- How the surroundings are described
- How Jane is affected by her fears

❸ Complete this table:

Point/detail	Evidence	Effect or explanation
1: *Thinking of her dead uncle turns Jane's thoughts to spirits and ghosts.*	*'I began to recall what I had heard of dead men … revisiting the earth'*	*Charlotte Brontë increases the tension as Jane describes ghostly actions in a long, breathless sentence.*
2: *A mysterious light increases her sense of horror.*		
3: *Jane's fear produces strong physical effects.*		

❹ Write up point 1 into a **paragraph** below, in your own words. Remember to include what you infer from the evidence, or the writer's effects.

....

....

....

....

....

❺ Now, choose **one** of your **other points** and write it out as another **paragraph** here:

....

....

....

....

....

....

....

PROGRESS LOG [tick the correct box]   Needs more work ☐   Getting there ☐   Under control ☐

Chapter 4: Jane meets Mr Brocklehurst

QUICK TEST ✔

1 Which of these statements about this chapter are **TRUE** and which are **FALSE**? Write **'T'** or **'F'** in the boxes:

a) Mrs Reed is persuaded to treat Jane kindly after her ordeal. ☐

b) Jane is excluded from the Reeds' Christmas celebrations. ☐

c) Jane is to be sent to a school called Lowood. ☐

d) Mr Brocklehurst is warm and friendly towards Jane. ☐

e) Jane is too afraid to speak her mind to Mrs Reed. ☐

f) By the end of the chapter Jane feels happy 'gleams of sunshine' in her life. ☐

THINKING MORE DEEPLY ?

2 Write **one or two sentences** in response to each of these questions:

a) How does Charlotte Brontë show that Jane has an independent spirit and the ability to stand up for what is right?

....

....

....

....

....

b) How does Charlotte Brontë present Mr Brocklehurst as a frightening person to Jane?

....

....

....

....

....

c) What do we learn of the relationship between Jane and Bessie by the end of the chapter?

....

....

....

....

....

EXAM PREPARATION: WRITING ABOUT TRUTHFULNESS AND DECEIT A01

Reread Jane's encounter with Mrs Reed from *'Speak I must'* (Ch. 4, p. 43) to *'You are deceitful!'* (p. 44).

Question: How is the theme of truthfulness and deceit developed in this passage?

Think about:

● What prompts Jane to tell the truth to Mrs Reed

● What the passage shows about the characters in it

3 Complete this table:

Point/detail	Evidence	Effect or explanation
1: *Jane speaks from a strong sense of injustice because Mrs Reed told Mr Brocklehurst she was deceitful.*	*'Speak I must: I had been trodden on severely, and must turn'*	*Jane's repetition of the word 'must' shows her conviction and the necessity to her of telling the truth.*
2: *Jane has the confidence to uphold what she knows is right.*		
3: *Charlotte Brontë makes the Reeds unattractive characters by showing that they are deceitful or hypocritical.*		

4 Write up point 1 into a **paragraph** below, in your own words. Remember to include what you infer from the evidence, or the writer's effects.

....

....

....

....

....

5 Now, choose **one** of your **other points** and write it out as another **paragraph** here:

....

....

....

....

PROGRESS LOG [tick the correct box]   Needs more work ☐   Getting there ☐   Under control ☐

Chapters 5–6: Jane's first days at Lowood School

QUICK TEST ✔

1 **Fill in the gaps** in these statements about events and characters in these chapters:

a) Jane travels alone to Lowood School on a cold day in the month of ....

b) Her first breakfast is a meal of burnt .... , which tastes so bad that she cannot eat it.

c) Jane admires the school's superintendent who is called ....

d) She sees a teacher called .... criticise and flog a girl unjustly.

e) Jane later talks to the girl and finds out that her name is ....

f) The school was founded as a charitable .... by a woman whose son, Mr Brocklehurst, is now in charge.

THINKING MORE DEEPLY ?

2 Write **one or two sentences** in response to each of these questions:

a) How does the description of life at Lowood create an impression of a harsh regime?

....
....
....
....
....

b) How does Helen Burns's attitude towards people who wrong her contrast with Jane's?

....
....
....
....
....

c) How does Charlotte Brontë present the character of Miss Temple?

....
....
....
....
....

EXAM PREPARATION: WRITING ABOUT NARRATIVE STRUCTURE

Reread from *'Is she going by herself?'* (Ch. 5, p. 50) to *'the coach instantly drove away'* (p. 51).

Question: How does Charlotte Brontë use this journey to convey a sense of Jane moving on to a new stage in her life?

Think about:

- How it shows Jane leaving Gateshead behind
- How it presents things that are new and different

3 Complete this table:

Point/detail	Evidence	Effect or explanation
1: *Jane is being sent away from everything she has known so far.*	*Jane describes being 'severed' from Bessie and Gateshead when the coach drives away.*	*Charlotte Brontë uses the word 'severed' to suggest a painful parting, and to signify the breaking of old ties.*
2: *She does not know what will happen in the next phase of her life.*		
3: *The unfamiliar towns and countryside give Jane an impression of great distance.*		

4 Write up **point 1** into a **paragraph** below in your own words. Remember to include what you infer from the evidence, or the writer's effects.

....

....

....

....

....

5 Now, choose **one** of your **other points** and write it out as another **paragraph** here:

....

....

....

....

....

....

PROGRESS LOG [tick the correct box]   Needs more work ☐   Getting there ☐   Under control ☐

Chapters 7–8: Life at Lowood and Jane's reputation restored

QUICK TEST ✔

1 **Number** the events of these two chapters so they are in the **correct sequence**. Use 1 for the first event and 7 for the final event.

a) Miss Temple comforts Jane, hears her story, and gives her and Helen tea and cake. ☐

b) Mr Brocklehurst tells the whole school what Mrs Reed told him – that Jane is a liar. ☐

c) Jane suffers at Lowood in the cold of the winter months. ☐

d) Mr Brocklehurst visits the school, inspecting and criticising the way it is run. ☐

e) By contacting Mr Lloyd, Miss Temple confirms the truth of Jane's story, and tells the school that her name has been cleared. ☐

f) Jane is punished by having to stand on a stool for an hour and having no one speak to her all day. ☐

g) Jane attracts Mr Brocklehurst's attention by accidentally dropping her slate. ☐

THINKING MORE DEEPLY ?

2 Write **one or two sentences** in response to each of these questions:

a) How does Charlotte Brontë's description of Sundays at Lowood contribute to ideas about religion in the novel?

....

....

....

....

b) How is the presentation of the Brocklehurst family ironic?

....

....

....

....

c) What is Helen Burns's influence on Jane?

....

....

....

....

EXAM PREPARATION: WRITING ABOUT A KEY MOMENT

Reread the end of Chapter 8 from *'About a week subsequently'* (Ch. 8, p. 88) to *'for Gateshead and its daily luxuries'* (p. 89).

Question: How is this passage important in the development of Jane's character?

Think about:

- The importance of Miss Temple's announcement
- Its effect on Jane's outlook and behaviour

3 Complete this table:

Point/detail	Evidence	Effect or explanation
1: *The restoration of her reputation is a very important event for Jane.*	*'Thus relieved of a grievous load'*	*Jane suffers the disgrace of being called a liar, and wants the people she likes to know her true moral worth.*
2: *With the injustices of Mrs Reed and Mr Brocklehurst behind her, Jane can now look forward in her new life.*		
3: *Jane realises the value of love in a poor environment over hatred and unhappiness in a rich one.*		

4 Write up **point 1** into a **paragraph** below in your own words. Remember to include what you infer from the evidence, or the writer's effects.

....

....

....

....

....

5 Now, choose **one** of your **other points** and write it out as another **paragraph** here:

....

....

....

....

....

....

PROGRESS LOG [tick the correct box]   Needs more work ☐   Getting there ☐   Under control ☐

Chapters 9–10: Helen dies and Jane becomes an adult

QUICK TEST ✔

1 Which of these statements about this chapter are **TRUE** and which are **FALSE**? Write **'T'** or **'F'** in the boxes:

a) An outbreak of typhus affects Lowood School killing many of its pupils. ☐

b) Jane enjoys greater freedom in the fine summer weather. ☐

c) She falls out with Helen Burns and finds a new friend. ☐

d) Jane stays at Lowood until the age of twenty-one. ☐

e) The reason she decides to leave Lowood is that Miss Temple has died. ☐

f) Jane receives an offer of a job as a governess at Thornfield. ☐

g) She is visited by Mrs Reed who gives her news of her cousins. ☐

THINKING MORE DEEPLY ?

2 Write **one or two sentences** in response to each of these questions:

a) What is the effect of the narrator's direct address to the reader, 'True, reader' (Ch. 9, p. 93)?

....

....

....

....

b) What ideas associated with the theme of religion are developed in the account of Helen's death?

....

....

....

....

c) How do the lives of the Reed children contrast with Jane's life at this stage in the story?

....

....

....

....

....

EXAM PREPARATION: WRITING ABOUT NATURE

Reread from *'Spring drew on'* (Ch. 9, p. 90) to *'which it now becomes my task to advert'* (p. 91).

Question: How does Charlotte Brontë use this description of nature to create a change of mood?

Think about:

- The language used to describe the natural world

- Jane's experience and emotions

3 Complete this table:

Point/detail	Evidence	Effect or explanation
1: *Charlotte Brontë makes a contrast between harsh winter and the softer spring.*	*'cutting winds' become 'gentler breathings'*	*Personification makes the world seem less hostile and cruel to Jane.*
2: *The imagery of life and death shows the difference between winter and spring.*		
3: *Jane enjoys the growing beauty around her.*		

4 Write up **point 1** into a **paragraph** below in your own words. Remember to include what you infer from the evidence, or the writer's effects.

....

....

....

....

5 Now, choose **one** of your **other points** and write it out as another **paragraph** here:

....

....

....

....

....

PROGRESS LOG [tick the correct box]   Needs more work ☐   Getting there ☐   Under control ☐

Chapter 11: Jane arrives at Thornfield Hall

QUICK TEST ✔

1 **Tick** the box for the correct answer to each of these questions.

a) What is Mrs Fairfax's attitude towards Jane when she arrives at Thornfield?

warm and welcoming ☐   distant and cold ☐   impatient and irritable ☐

b) What is Mrs Fairfax's position at Thornfield?

owner ☐   housekeeper ☐   governess ☐

c) What is Adèle's relationship to Mr Rochester?

niece ☐   daughter ☐   ward ☐

d) Where is Thornfield Hall?

six miles from Millcote ☐   near Lowton ☐   in the town of Millcote ☐

e) Who does Mrs Fairfax say is responsible for the strange laughter that Jane hears?

Leah ☐   Adèle ☐   Grace Poole ☐

THINKING MORE DEEPLY ❓

2 Write **one or two sentences** in response to each of these questions:

a) What are Jane's feelings as she waits for the carriage to take her to Thornfield Hall?

....

....

....

....

b) How does Jane describe her own appearance?

....

....

....

....

c) What information does Jane receive about Mr Rochester?

....

....

....

....

EXAM PREPARATION: WRITING ABOUT THE PRESENTATION OF SETTING A02

Reread from *'When we left the dining-room'* (Ch. 11, p. 124) to *'they rest tranquilly in their graves now'* (p. 125).

Question: How does Charlotte Brontë present Thornfield Hall?

Think about:

- How she creates an impression of grandeur and age
- Its atmosphere and effect on Jane

3 Complete this table:

Point/detail	Evidence	Effect or explanation
1: *Jane admires the house as she follows Mrs Fairfax.*	*Charlotte Brontë uses adjectives such as 'grand', 'handsome' and 'venerable'.*	*This setting makes a strong contrast with the simplicity of Lowood, and the change marks a new phase in Jane's life.*
2: *The age of the house is emphasised by what Jane sees.*		
3: *The house has an air of gloom associated with death and a hint of horror.*		

4 Write up **point 1** into a **paragraph** below in your own words. Remember to include what you infer from the evidence, or the writer's effects.

....
....
....
....
....

5 Now, choose **one** of your **other points** and write it out as another **paragraph** here:

....
....
....
....
....
....

PROGRESS LOG [tick the correct box]   Needs more work ☐   Getting there ☐   Under control ☐

Chapters 12–14: Jane meets and talks to Mr Rochester

QUICK TEST ✔

1 Complete this **gap-fill paragraph** about events in Chapter 12 with the correct or suitable information:

By the start of Chapter 12 Jane has been at Thornfield for .... months. Wanting a change of scene, she walks to the nearby village of .... to post a letter. Hearing a horse approaching she thinks of a mythical creature called a .... The horse slips on .... and the rider falls, spraining his ankle. Jane helps him and then continues on her way. When Jane returns to Thornfield she discovers that the rider was ....

THINKING MORE DEEPLY ?

2 Write **one or two sentences** in response to each of these questions:

a) Why does Jane feel restless in spite of her happiness at Thornfield Hall?

....

....

....

....

b) What sort of atmosphere does Charlotte Brontë create around Jane's first meeting with Mr Rochester?

....

....

....

....

c) What impression of Mr Rochester is created by Mrs Fairfax's account of his background?

....

....

....

....

EXAM PREPARATION: WRITING ABOUT SOCIAL CONVENTIONS — A03

Reread Jane's conversation with Mr Rochester from *'I am willing to amuse you, if I can'* (Ch. 14, p. 156) to *'nothing free-born would submit to, even for a salary'* (p. 158).

Question: How does this passage develop ideas about equality?

Think about:

- Mr Rochester's view of his rights over Jane
- Jane's opinion and response to him

3 Complete this table:

Point/detail	Evidence	Effect or explanation
1: *Mr Rochester believes that his age and experience entitle him to command Jane, but she wisely disagrees.*	*'your claim to superiority depends on the use you have made of your time and experience.'*	*Once again, Jane expresses her independent thoughts which challenge the conventional hierarchy in society.*
2: *Jane likes Mr Rochester because he seems to forget his rights as her employer, and treats her equally.*		
3: *They speak honestly and informally to each other.*		

4 Write up **point 1** into a **paragraph** below in your own words. Remember to include what you infer from the evidence, or the writer's effects.

....

....

....

....

....

5 Now, choose **one** of your **other points** and write it out as another **paragraph** here.

....

....

....

....

....

....

PROGRESS LOG [tick the correct box]   Needs more work ☐   Getting there ☐   Under control ☐

Chapters 15–16: Jane saves Rochester's life

QUICK TEST ✔

1 Which of these statements about these chapters are **TRUE** and which are **FALSE**? Write **'T'** or **'F'** in the boxes:

a) Mr Rochester admits the mistakes he made in his relationship with Celine Varens. ☐

b) Jane does not like hearing about Mr Rochester's experiences. ☐

c) Jane sees only goodness in Mr Rochester's character. ☐

d) On the morning after the fire, Mr Rochester gives Jane a full explanation for it. ☐

e) Jane believes that Grace Poole is hiding the facts from her. ☐

f) Jane believes that Mr Rochester will marry Blanche Ingram. ☐

g) Jane cannot control her feelings of disappointment at the end of Chapter 16. ☐

THINKING MORE DEEPLY ❓

2 Write **one or two sentences** in response to each of these questions:

a) How does Jane respond when she learns that Adèle is 'the illegitimate offspring of a French opera-girl' (Ch. 15, p. 170)?

....

....

....

....

b) How does Charlotte Brontë's language make the incident of the fire dramatic?

....

....

....

....

....

c) In what ways is Blanche Ingram different from Jane?

....

....

....

....

EXAM PREPARATION: WRITING ABOUT JANE'S INNER VOICE

Reread Jane's words to herself from *'That a greater fool than Jane Eyre'* (Ch. 16, p. 186) to *'I grew calm, and fell asleep'* (p. 187).

Question: How does this passage show Jane's ability to control her emotions?

Think about:

- The feelings Jane expresses
- The language she uses to reproach herself

3 Complete this table:

Point/detail	Evidence	Effect or explanation
1: Jane feels foolish and embarrassed that she thought Mr Rochester admired her.	She describes herself as a 'fantastic idiot' and questions herself three times.	The rhetorical questions which mockingly use the pronoun 'you' show Jane's ability to consider critically her own behaviour.
2: She includes advice about women's experience.		
3: She severely imposes a punishment on herself as a reminder of her foolishness.		

4 Write up **point 1** into a **paragraph** below in your own words. Remember to include what you infer from the evidence, or the writer's effects.

....

....

....

....

....

5 Now, choose **one** of your **other points** and write it out as another **paragraph** here:

....

....

....

....

....

....

PROGRESS LOG [tick the correct box]   Needs more work ☐   Getting there ☐   Under control ☐

Chapters 17–19: Visitors at Thornfield Hall

QUICK TEST ✔

1 **Number** the events of these chapters so that they are in the **correct sequence**. Use 1 for the first event and 7 for the final event.

a) Jane overhears a mysterious conversation about Grace Poole and her role at Thornfield. ☐

b) A fortune-teller seems to understand Jane's position and character. ☐

c) Mr Rochester seems disturbed when he hears of Mr Mason's arrival. ☐

d) Jane feels uncomfortable when Mr Rochester makes her join the party after dinner. ☐

e) Mr Rochester reveals himself in disguise to Jane. ☐

f) Mr Rochester returns to Thornfield with a party of guests. ☐

g) A stranger called Mr Mason arrives at Thornfield when Mr Rochester is out. ☐

THINKING MORE DEEPLY ?

2 Write **one or two sentences** in response to each of these questions:

a) How does Charlotte Brontë convey the impression in Chapter 17 that the relationship between Mr Rochester and Blanche Ingram is only superficial?

....

....

....

....

b) How does Charlotte Brontë reveal Mr Rochester's feelings for Jane at the end of Chapter 17?

....

....

....

....

c) How does Mr Rochester react to the news that a visitor called Mr Mason has arrived?

....

....

....

....

....

EXAM PREPARATION: WRITING ABOUT BLANCHE INGRAM

Reread the conversation about governesses started by Blanche Ingram from *'I have just one word to say of the whole tribe'* (Ch. 17, p. 205) to *'My lily-flower, you are right now, as always'* (p. 206).

Question: How does Charlotte Brontë use this conversation to reveal the character of Blanche Ingram?

Think about:

- How Blanche reports her treatment of her governess
- Her attitude towards other characters

3 Complete this table:

Point/detail	Evidence	Effect or explanation
1: *Blanche enjoys entertaining others with details of how she tormented her governess and her brother's tutor.*	*'when we had driven her to extremities'* *'I helped you in … persecuting'*	*The verb 'persecuting' reveals a spiteful character who despises her inferiors. She is insensitive to Jane's presence in the room.*
2: *She and her brother boast of publicly shaming the governess and tutor over their relationship.*		
3: *Blanche is rude to her mother in public.*		

4 Write up **point 1** into a **paragraph** below in your own words. Remember to include what you infer from the evidence, or the writer's effects.

....
....
....
....

5 Now, choose **one** of your **other points** and write it out as another **paragraph** here:

....
....
....
....
....

PROGRESS LOG [tick the correct box]   Needs more work ☐   Getting there ☐   Under control ☐

Chapters 20–22: Drama at Thornfield and a visit to the Reeds

QUICK TEST ✔

1 **Tick** the box for the correct answer to each of these questions:

a) What does Jane think has caused Mr Mason's injuries?

He was bitten by Pilot ☐   He fell off his horse ☐

He was attacked by Grace Poole ☐

b) Who unexpectedly visits Jane at Thornfield?

Bessie's husband, Robert ☐   John Reed ☐   Mr Mason ☐

c) Where does Jane go to visit?

Lowood School ☐   Gateshead Hall ☐   Millcote ☐

d) How does Jane respond to Mrs Reed?

with forgiveness ☐   with resentment ☐   with anger ☐

e) Where does Jane meet Mr Rochester on her return to Thornfield?

in the library ☐   in the garden ☐   at a stile ☐

THINKING MORE DEEPLY ❓

2 Write **one or two sentences** in response to each of these questions:

a) How does Charlotte Brontë convey a sense of Gothic horror as Jane sits with Mr Mason?

....

....

....

....

b) What does Mrs Reed confess to Jane?

....

....

....

....

c) What impression is created of Eliza and Georgiana Reed?

....

....

....

....

EXAM PREPARATION: WRITING ABOUT NARRATIVE TECHNIQUE A02

Reread the account of Jane's journey back to Thornfield from *'I had not notified to Mrs Fairfax'* (Ch. 22, p. 280) to *'a book and pencil in his hand; he is writing'* (p. 281).

Question: How does Charlotte Brontë's narrative technique make this passage effective?

Think about:

● The description of the weather and scene

● The voice of the narrator

3 Complete this table:

Point/detail	Evidence	Effect or explanation
1: *The weather is conveyed through vivid detail.*	*The colours are attractive: 'blue' and 'golden redness', and the clouds are not threatening.*	*The weather acts as a metaphor for Jane's mood – 'I felt glad' – as she returns to Mr Rochester.*
2: *Charlotte Brontë reminds the reader that the story is being told by the older Jane looking back on her life.*		
3: *As Jane approaches Thornfield and sees Mr Rochester, there is a shift to the present tense.*		

4 Write up **point 1** into a **paragraph** below in your own words. Remember to include what you infer from the evidence, or the writer's effects.

....
....
....
....
....

5 Now, choose **one** of your **other points** and write it out as another **paragraph** here:

....
....
....
....
....
....

PROGRESS LOG [tick the correct box]   Needs more work ☐   Getting there ☐   Under control ☐

Chapter 23: Rochester proposes

QUICK TEST ✔

① **Complete** this **gap-fill paragraph** about events in Chapter 23 with the correct or suitable information:

On a beautiful .... evening Jane decides to walk in the ....
where she meets Mr Rochester. He talks about finding her another position as
a governess in ...., and Jane is forced to admit that the prospect of
leaving him seems like .... Mr Rochester denies that he will marry
..............................., and proposes to Jane. As she accepts his proposal, the
weather becomes .... Later, the tree under which they stood is struck
by ....

THINKING MORE DEEPLY ❓

② Write **one or two sentences** in response to each of these questions:

a) How does Charlotte Brontë describe a beautiful scene at the opening of this chapter?

....
....
....
....
....

b) How does Charlotte Brontë suggest to the reader that Rochester is only teasing Jane when he tells her about the position in Ireland?

....
....
....
....
....

c) How does the change in the weather create a sense of foreboding?

....
....
....
....
....

EXAM PREPARATION: WRITING ABOUT THE LANGUAGE OF ARGUMENT A02

Reread from *'I tell you I must go'* (Ch. 23, p. 292) to *'my … best earthly companion'* (p. 293).

Question: How does Charlotte Brontë reveal Jane's strong character in this passage?

Think about:

● Jane's principles and opinions

● The power of her language

Complete this table:

Point/detail	Evidence	Effect or explanation
1: *Jane regards herself as Rochester's equal, and even morally superior to him.*	*'equal – as we are'* *'I would scorn such a union: therefore I am better than you'*	*Jane believes that her strength comes from her moral character – and this sets her above others with wealth and power, like Rochester.*
2: *She is brave and confident in expressing her feelings.*		
3: *Jane's speech has rhetorical impact.*		

❹ Write up **point 1** into a **paragraph** below in your own words. Remember to include what you infer from the evidence, or the writer's effects.

....

....

....

....

....

❺ Now, choose **one** of your **other points** and write it out as another **paragraph** here:

....

....

....

....

....

....

PROGRESS LOG [tick the correct box]   Needs more work ☐   Getting there ☐   Under control ☐

Chapters 24–25: Wedding plans and a hint of danger

QUICK TEST ✔

1 Which of these statements about these chapters are **TRUE** and which are **FALSE**?
Write **'T'** or **'F'** in the boxes:

a) Mr Rochester wants to shower Jane with jewels and rich clothes. ☐

b) Jane is happy to accept all that Mr Rochester gives her. ☐

c) Jane feels she will never need an independent income of her own. ☐

d) She writes a letter to her uncle, John Eyre to tell him that she is still alive. ☐

e) She has a lovely dream of happiness and security at Thornfield. ☐

f) Jane fully accepts Rochester's explanation of the visitor in her room. ☐

g) She spends a sleepless night in Adèle's room before the wedding. ☐

THINKING MORE DEEPLY ?

2 Write **one or two sentences** in response to each of these questions:

a) What does Mr Rochester value in Jane?

....

....

....

....

....

b) What fears does Mrs Fairfax express about the relationship between Jane
and Rochester?

....

....

....

....

....

c) How does the weather reflect Jane's mood as she waits for Rochester in
Chapter 25?

....

....

....

....

....

EXAM PREPARATION: WRITING ABOUT EFFECTS

Reread Jane's account of the events of the night before her wedding from *'On waking, a gleam dazzled my eyes'* (Ch. 25, p. 326) to *'I became insensible from terror'* (p. 327).

Question: How does Charlotte Brontë's use of language in this account create an impression of horror?

Think about:

- The choice of imagery
- The sense of mystery

③ Complete this table:

Point/detail	Evidence	Effect /exploration
1: *Charlotte Brontë uses light and dark to create the horror of a scene taking place at dead of night.*	*'only candle-light'* *'perhaps it saw dawn approaching'*	*Darkness traditionally symbolises confusion and the emergence of evil. The figure withdraws when it senses dawn approaching.*
2: *Jane describes how her fear affects her physically.*		
3: *Mystery surrounds the visitor in spite of Jane's attempts to identify it rationally.*		

④ Write up **point 1** into a **paragraph** below in your own words. Remember to include what you infer from the evidence, or the writer's effects.

....

....

....

....

....

⑤ Now, choose **one** of your **other points** and write it out as another **paragraph** here:

....

....

....

....

....

....

PROGRESS LOG [tick the correct box]   Needs more work ☐   Getting there ☐   Under control ☐

Chapters 26–27: The marriage is prevented and Jane flees

QUICK TEST ✓

1 **Number** the events of these chapters so that they are in the **correct sequence**.
Use 1 for the first event and 7 for the final event.

a) Having determined to follow her religious and moral principles,
Jane secretly leaves Thornfield before dawn the next day. ☐

b) They all return to Thornfield where Rochester reveals Bertha locked
upstairs with Grace Poole. ☐

c) Rochester hurries Jane to the church for their wedding early in
the morning. ☐

d) One of the strangers interrupts the ceremony, saying there is an
impediment to the marriage. ☐

e) Jane notices two strangers quietly enter the church. ☐

f) Rochester explains the circumstances of his marriage and begs
Jane to stay. ☐

g) The strangers are revealed to be Mr Mason and his lawyer, who say
that Mr Rochester is already married to Mason's sister. ☐

THINKING MORE DEEPLY ?

2 Write **one or two sentences** in response to each of these questions:

a) How does the opening of Chapter 26 show Rochester's impatience?

....

....

....

....

b) How does Charlotte Brontë show once again John Eyre's significance in Jane's life?

....

....

....

....

c) How does Charlotte Brontë use metaphors on Chapter 27, page 366 to express
the strength of Jane's character?

....

....

....

....

Reread the description of Bertha Rochester from *'He lifted the hangings'* (Ch. 26, p. 338) to *'a smile both acrid and desolate' (p.* 339).

Question: What impressions of Bertha's character are conveyed by Charlotte Brontë's choice of language?

Think about:

- The words used to refer to her
- Her appearance and behaviour

❸ Complete this table:

Point/detail	Evidence	Effect or explanation
1: *Charlotte Brontë makes Bertha seem like an animal.*	*'like some strange wild animal'* *'it snatched and growled'* *'hair, wild as a mane'*	*The simile and the pronoun 'it' dehumanise Bertha. The verbs describing her actions and the noun 'mane' are words that we associate with wild animals.*
2: *Bertha is shown as big, strong and violent.*		
3: *Bertha is cunning and dangerous.*		

❹ Write up **point 1** into a **paragraph** below in your own words. Remember to include what you infer from the evidence, or the writer's effects.

....

....

....

....

....

❺ Now, choose **one** of your **other points** and write it out as another **paragraph** here:

....

....

....

....

....

....

....

PROGRESS LOG [tick the correct box]　　Needs more work ☐　　Getting there ☐　　Under control ☐

Chapters 28–31: Jane starts a new life

QUICK TEST ✔

1 **Tick** the box for the correct answer to each of these questions:

a) For how long does Jane wander through the countryside alone?

one day ☐   three days ☐   a week ☐

b) What prevents Jane from begging for food?

She is too proud ☐   She is afraid ☐   She is too weak ☐

c) Who shows pity by taking her into a house?

Hannah ☐   St John Rivers ☐   Diana ☐

d) What disappointing news do the Rivers family receive in Chapter 30?

They have to leave their house ☐

They have been excluded from their uncle's will ☐   Their father has died ☐

e) What job is Jane offered?

governess in London ☐   seamstress ☐   teacher in a village school ☐

f) Who is the beautiful daughter of a wealthy factory owner whom St John loves?

Mary Rivers ☐   Rosamund Oliver ☐   Hannah Morton ☐

THINKING MORE DEEPLY ?

2 Write **one or two sentences** in response to each of these questions:

a) Why does Jane say that she is called Elliott instead of giving her real name?

....

....

....

....

b) How does Jane feel about Diana and Mary?

....

....

....

....

c) How do these chapters develop the theme of education?

....

....

....

....

EXAM PREPARATION: WRITING ABOUT JANE'S CHARACTER (A01) ✎

Reread Jane's account of her feelings about her work from *'Was I very gleeful'* (Ch. 31, p. 414) to *'I thank His providence for the guidance!'* (p. 414).

Question: How does Charlotte Brontë use this internal monologue to reveal Jane's character?

Think about:

- The feelings she expresses
- The underlying principles she reveals

③ Complete this table:

Point/detail	Evidence	Effect or explanation
1: Jane describes her feelings truthfully, the bad as well as the good.	*'Not to deceive myself, I must reply – no'*	*Yet again, Jane has the courage to face the truth, however uncomfortable it may be.*
2: She is resilient and hopeful, proud of the choice she has made.		
3: Her actions are based on religious principles.		

④ Write up **point 1** into a **paragraph** below in your own words. Remember to include what you infer from the evidence, or the writer's effects.

....

....

....

....

⑤ Now, choose **one** of your **other points** and write it out as another **paragraph** here:

....

....

....

....

....

PROGRESS LOG [tick the correct box]   Needs more work ☐   Getting there ☐   Under control ☐

Chapters 32–33: St John's feelings and Jane's inheritance

QUICK TEST

1 Complete this **gap-fill paragraph** about events in these chapters with the correct or suitable information.

Jane is painting a picture of .... when St John arrives at her cottage. It prompts a conversation in which he admits that he .... but will not marry Rosamund. St John notices and tears off a .... scribbled on Jane's drawing paper. He leaves hurriedly. The next day, St John struggles through a .... to visit Jane again and tell her that he knows the truth about her. He reveals that she has inherited .... from her uncle ...., who is also uncle to him and his sisters. Jane is delighted to find she has a ...., and insists on sharing the inheritance with them.

THINKING MORE DEEPLY ?

2 Write **one or two sentences** in response to each of these questions:

a) What pleasure does Jane find in her new life and work?

....
....
....
....

b) What are St John's reasons for not marrying Rosamund?

....
....
....
....

c) What are Jane's reasons for sharing her inheritance with St John, Diana and Mary?

....
....
....
....

EXAM PREPARATION: WRITING ABOUT A TURNING POINT IN THE STORY (A01)

Reread the end of Chapter 32 from *'Having said this'* (p. 433) to *'and soon forgot it'* (p. 434).

Question: How does this passage suggest that the plot is going to take a major leap forward?

Think about:

- St John's sudden change of mood
- How Charlotte Brontë creates a mystery

Complete this table:

Point/detail	Evidence	Effect or explanation
1: *St John's attention is dramatically shifted.*	*Charlotte Brontë refers to the apparently 'blank paper' and his urgent action: 'with a snatch … shot a glance'.*	*He suddenly stops talking about Rosamund and focuses on an unexplained detail, building a sense of mystery.*
2: *St John's behaviour is secretive and mysterious.*		
3: *The chapter ends without explanation, creating a kind of cliff-hanger.*		

④ Write up **point 1** into a **paragraph** below in your own words. Remember to include what you infer from the evidence, or the writer's effects.

....

....

....

....

⑤ Now, choose **one** of your **other points** and write it out as another **paragraph** here:

....

....

....

....

....

....

PROGRESS LOG [tick the correct box]   Needs more work ☐   Getting there ☐   Under control ☐

Chapters 34–35: St John proposes but Jane hears Rochester's call

QUICK TEST ✔

1 Which of these statements about these chapters are **TRUE** and which are **FALSE**?
Write **'T'** or **'F'** in the boxes:

a) Jane takes great pleasure in preparing Moor House for Diana and
Mary's return. ☐

b) St John is pleased by the comfort that Jane's new circumstances
have brought her. ☐

c) St John asks Jane to learn a language so that she will be useful to him. ☐

d) Jane feels stifled by St John. ☐

e) Jane forgets about Rochester. ☐

f) St John proposes to Jane because he loves her. ☐

g) Diana approves of her brother's wishes. ☐

THINKING MORE DEEPLY ?

2 Write **one or two sentences** in response to each of these questions:

a) What are Jane's reasons for agreeing to consider accompanying St John
to India?

....

....

....

....

b) Why does St John insist that they should be married if Jane accompanies him?

....

....

....

....

....

c) What comparisons does Jane make between St John and Rochester?

....

....

....

....

EXAM PREPARATION: WRITING ABOUT THE LANGUAGE OF PASSION   A02

Reread Jane's description of hearing Rochester's call from *'I contended with my inward dimness of vision'* (Ch. 35, p. 482) to *'moorland loneliness and midnight hush'* (p. 483).

Question: How does Charlotte Brontë use language in this passage to convey Jane's strong emotions?

Think about:

● What Jane's emotions are

● The images Charlotte Brontë uses to express them

③ Complete this table:

Point/detail	Evidence	Effect or explanation
1: *At first, the scene around Jane is motionless and quiet.*	*'All the house was still'*	*The stillness creates an air of expectancy and heightens our sense of the turbulence of Jane's emotions by creating a contrast.*
2: *Jane's emotions affect her intensely.*		
3: *The pace of the passage changes to reflect what is happening.*		

④ Write up **point 1** into a **paragraph** below in your own words. Remember to include what you infer from the evidence, or the writer's effects.

....

....

....

....

....

⑤ Now, choose **one** of your **other points** and write it out as another **paragraph** here:

....

....

....

....

....

....

PROGRESS LOG [tick the correct box]   Needs more work ☐   Getting there ☐   Under control ☐

Chapters 36–38: Jane returns to Thornfield and Rochester

QUICK TEST ✔

1 **Number** the events of these chapters so that they are in the **correct sequence**. Use 1 for the first event and 7 for the final event.

a) With ten years of happy marriage behind her, Jane gives details of what has happened to all the other characters. ☐

b) Jane goes to Ferndean where she and Rochester are reunited. ☐

c) She is shocked to find Thornfield a 'blackened ruin' (Ch. 36, p. 489). ☐

d) Jane retraces her steps back to Thornfield, delighting in familiar scenes. ☐

e) The innkeeper tells Jane that Rochester lost his sight and one of his hands in the fire, and now lives alone at Ferndean Manor. ☐

f) The innkeeper tells Jane that Bertha Rochester started a fire before throwing herself off the battlements to her death. ☐

g) After hearing Jane's story of the last few months, Rochester proposes to her and she accepts him. ☐

THINKING MORE DEEPLY ?

2 Write **one or two sentences** in response to each of these questions:

a) How does Charlotte Brontë show that Rochester is a reformed character at the end of the novel?

b) What do we learn about the fates of other characters at the end of the novel?

c) How is the theme of religion developed in these final chapters?

EXAM PREPARATION: WRITING ABOUT SETTING

Reread the description of Ferndean Manor from *'To this house I came just ere dark'* (Ch. 37, p. 496) to *'audible in its vicinage'* (p. 497).

Question: How does the imagery used to describe this setting convey Mr Rochester's mood and situation?

Think about:

- The mood of the setting and its links with Rochester
- How Charlotte Brontë uses language to convey atmosphere

3 Complete this table:

Point/ detail	Evidence	Effect or explanation
1: *Charlotte Brontë immediately establishes a mood of unhappiness.*	*'sad sky'* *'gloomy wood'* *'a desolate spot'*	*Following the innkeeper's account of all that has happened to Rochester, the adjectives 'sad', 'gloomy' and 'desolate' seem to reflect his present mood and situation.*
2: *Charlotte Brontë uses light and dark to convey Rochester's moods in Chapter 37.*		
3: *The natural world seems to put barriers in Jane's way.*		

4 Write up **point 1** into a **paragraph** below in your own words. Remember to include what you infer from the evidence, or the writer's effects.

....

....

....

....

....

5 Now, choose **one** of your **other points** and write it out as another **paragraph** here:

....

....

....

....

....

....

PROGRESS LOG [tick the correct box]   Needs more work ☐   Getting there ☐   Under control ☐

Practice task

1 First, **read** this **exam-style** task:

Jane is making her way back to Thornfield after hearing Mr. Rochester's call.

Reread from: *'I left Moor House at three o' clock'* (Ch. 36, p.487) to *'I was already on my master's very lands.'* (p. 487).

Question: How does Charlotte Brontë use journeys to further the plot and develop Jane's story?

Think about:

- How the journey is used in this extract
- How journeys are used in the novel as a whole

2 Begin by circling the **key words** in the **question** above.

3 Now complete the table, noting down **three or four key points** with **evidence** and the **effect** created.

Point	Evidence/quotation	Effect or explanation

4 **Draft your response**. Use the space below for your first paragraph(s) and then continue onto a sheet of paper.

Start: *In this journey, as Jane approaches the end of her story, Charlotte Brontë conveys a sense of anticipation by …* ....

....

....

....

....

PROGRESS LOG [tick the correct box]   Needs more work ☐   Getting there ☐   Under control ☐

Who's who?

1 Look at the drawings below. **Complete** the **name** of each of the characters and/or **who** they are in the novel.

Name: Jane Eyre

Who: ....

Name: ....

Who: Jane's husband (at the end)

Name: Mrs ....

Who: Jane's aunt and legal guardian

Name: ....

Who: Jane's school friend

Name: Mr Brocklehurst

Who: ....
....

Name: Mrs Fairfax

Who: ....
....

Name: Blanche Ingram

Who: ....
....

Names: ....
and .... Rivers

Who: Jane's rescuers and cousins

2 Which major and minor characters are missing from the section above? Fill in the table below:

Characters at Gateshead Hall	Characters at Lowood School	Characters at Thornfield	Others?

PROGRESS LOG [tick the correct box]   Needs more work ☐   Getting there ☐   Under control ☐

Jane Eyre

1 Look at this bank of **adjectives**. Circle the ones that you think best **describe** Jane:

> *beautiful   sly   truthful   spiteful   passionate   affectionate*
>
> *brave   selfish   resilient   weak   lazy   artistic*
>
> *hard-working   imaginative   loyal   principled*

2 Write down **two pieces of evidence** to support each of these statements about Jane:

a) She has the courage to act independently.

1: ....

2: ....

b) She has unconventional views about social status.

1: ....

2: ....

c) She stands up for justice.

1: ....

2: ....

3 **Complete these statements** about Charlotte Brontë's presentation of Jane using your own judgement:

a) Charlotte Brontë makes the reader feel sympathy for Jane by …

....

....

....

b) Charlotte Brontë suggests that Jane has a strong / weak Christian faith by …

....

....

....

c) In my opinion, Charlotte Brontë gives Jane a happy ending to show that …

....

....

....

PROGRESS LOG [tick the correct box]   Needs more work ☐   Getting there ☐   Under control ☐

Mr Rochester

1 Without looking at the book, **write down from memory** at least two details that Charlotte Brontë uses to present Mr Rochester in each of these ways:

As a dark and passionate romantic hero	
As a man troubled by his past	
As courageous and honourable	

2 **Write a comment** on Charlotte Brontë's use of language in this quotation paying attention to the underlined phrases:

'He rose and came towards me, and I saw his face <u>all kindled</u>, and his full <u>falcon-eye</u> <u>flashing</u>, and <u>tenderness and passion</u> in every lineament.' **(Ch. 24, p. 314)**

....
....
....
....
....
....

3 Write two sentences in response to each of these questions:

a) What faults does Charlotte Brontë present in Mr Rochester's character?

....
....
....
....

b) How is Mr Rochester redeemed at the end of the novel?

....
....
....
....
....

PROGRESS LOG [tick the correct box]   Needs more work ☐   Getting there ☐   Under control ☐

Bertha Rochester

1 Look at these statements about Bertha. For each one, decide whether it is **True [T]**, **False [F]** or whether there is **Not Enough Evidence [NEE]** to decide:

a) Bertha was a wealthy heiress from Jamaica. [T] [F] [NEE]

b) Rochester was persuaded to marry her by his father and brother. [T] [F] [NEE]

c) Bertha loves Rochester very deeply. [T] [F] [NEE]

d) She is cared for at Thornfield by Mrs Fairfax. [T] [F] [NEE]

e) She attacks her brother Richard Mason when he visits Thornfield. [T] [F] [NEE]

f) She starts a fire in Jane's bed that destroys Thornfield. [T] [F] [NEE]

g) Mr Rochester kills her. [T] [F] [NEE]

2 Circle the correct word or phrase to **complete** these statements about Bertha's significance in the novel:

a) Charlotte Brontë uses Bertha as [a theme / an idea / a plot device] whose actions drive the plot forward.

b) Bertha contributes to the sense of [Gothic mystery and threat / domestic bliss / superstition] that Jane experiences at Thornfield Hall.

c) Bertha provides the [challenge / conflict / question] which must be resolved in order for Jane and Rochester to be together.

3 **Give three examples** of the ways in which Charlotte Brontë presents Bertha as the **antithesis or opposite** of Jane.

1: ....

....

2: ....

....

3: ....

....

4 Using your **own judgement**, put a mark along this line to show **Brontë's overall presentation** of Bertha.

Not at all sympathetic	A little sympathetic	Quite sympathetic	Very sympathetic
①	②	③	④

PROGRESS LOG [tick the correct box]　　Needs more work ☐　　Getting there ☐　　Under control ☐

St John Rivers

1 **Complete these quotations,** which are either what St John says or what others say about him.

a) Jane describes him as, 'a .... man: tall, fair, with blue eyes, and a .... profile'.

b) Jane says his appearance 'indicated elements within either restless or ...., or eager'.

c) Diana says 'in some things he is inexorable as .... '.

d) St John says, 'A .... I resolved to be.'

e) St John says, 'while I love Rosamund Oliver so wildly [...] she would not make me a good .... '.

f) St John describes his vocation as: 'My .... work? My foundation laid on earth for a mansion in ....?'.

2 **Complete these statements** about St John:

a) Charlotte Brontë uses St John to move the plot forward when he discovers ....

....

b) St John wants Jane to marry him so that ....

....

c) St John's attitude to religious belief is ....

....

3 **Add a tick after each statement** to indicate whether it applies to St John or Rochester.

Statement	St John	Rochester
He loves Jane passionately.		
He holds great influence over her and she works hard to please him.		
He is not conventionally attractive.		
He is willing to break the law to get what he wants.		
He actively helps other people.		
He puts religious principles before his personal happiness.		

PROGRESS LOG [tick the correct box]   Needs more work ☐   Getting there ☐   Under control ☐

Mrs Reed

❶ Look at this bank of **adjectives**. Circle the ones that you think **best describe** Mrs Reed:

powerful	kind	compassionate	proud	loving	indulgent	unfair
resentful	remorseful	wealthy	intimidating	sympathetic		hard
respectable	cruel	deceitful	generous	regretful	vindictive	

❷ Write one or two sentences explaining how each of these characters is linked to Mrs Reed and affected by her:

a) John Reed is ....

....

....

b) Jane Eyre is ....

....

....

c) John Eyre is ....

....

....

❸ **Complete this table** to show how Charlotte Brontë's presentation of Mrs Reed contributes to important **themes** in the novel:

Theme	Evidence of Mrs Reed's connection with it	How this contributes to or develops the theme
Childhood		
Justice		
Christian duty		

PROGRESS LOG [tick the correct box]   Needs more work ☐   Getting there ☐   Under control ☐

Helen Burns

1 Look at these statements about Helen Burns. For each one, decide whether it is
True [T], False [F] or whether there is **Not Enough Evidence [NEE]** to decide:

a) Jane meets Helen at Gateshead.   [T] [F] [NEE]

b) Helen is flogged by Miss Scatcherd.   [T] [F] [NEE]

c) Helen resents the treatment she receives.   [T] [F] [NEE]

d) She would like to be a missionary.   [T] [F] [NEE]

e) She has a strong Christian faith.   [T] [F] [NEE]

f) She dies of tuberculosis.   [T] [F] [NEE]

g) She is intelligent and well read.   [T] [F] [NEE]

2 **Complete these statements** about Helen Burns:

a) Even though Jane admires her, Helen recognises her own faults such as ....

....

b) Helen describes Miss Temple as ....

....

c) Jane creates a memorial to Helen by ....

....

3 **Complete this table** to show how Helen expresses **different views** from Jane on
some important issues in Chapter 6:

	Helen's view	Jane's view
Miss Scatcherd		
Treatment of others		
Holding a grudge		

PROGRESS LOG [tick the correct box]   Needs more work ☐   Getting there ☐   Under control ☐

Miss Temple

1 Without looking at the book, **write down from memory** at least one piece of evidence to support each of these statements about Miss Temple:

Statement	Evidence
She is not afraid of Mr Brocklehurst.	
She cares about her students' welfare.	
She is particularly fond of Helen Burns.	
She is active in seeking justice for Jane.	

2 **Complete this table** comparing **Miss Temple** and **Diana Rivers** who are similar, influential female characters in Jane's story:

	Miss Temple	Diana Rivers
Appearance		
Education		
Jane's feelings towards them		

3 **Write a paragraph** to explain how Charlotte Brontë uses Miss Temple to **advance the plot**. You could start like this: *Miss Temple's departure from Lowood...*

....

....

....

....

....

....

....

PROGRESS LOG [tick the correct box]   Needs more work ☐   Getting there ☐   Under control ☐

Mr Brocklehurst, Mrs Fairfax, Grace Poole

1 Which character? **Tick** the character that each quotation refers to:

Quotation	Mr Brocklehurst	Mrs Fairfax	Grace Poole
'a black pillar … straight, narrow, sable-clad shape'			
'as companionless as a prisoner in his dungeon'			
'My heart really warmed to the worthy lady'			
'it is not every one could fill her shoes – not for all the money she gets'			
'a placid-tempered, kind-natured woman'			
'a harsh man; at once pompous and meddling'			

2 **Write at least one sentence** in response to each of these questions:

a) How does Charlotte Brontë suggest that Mr Brocklehurst is hypocritical?

....

....

b) How does Mrs Fairfax react to the news of Jane's marriage to Rochester?

....

....

c) What is the 'fault' in Grace that occasionally leads to Bertha's escape?

....

....

3 **Use your own judgement** to write a paragraph on a separate piece of paper about how Charlotte Brontë uses each of these characters to develop an idea or theme:

a) Mr Brocklehurst and religion

b) Mrs Fairfax and social status

c) Grace Poole and Gothic horror

Diana and Mary Rivers, Blanche Ingram

1 How do these three **characters behave**? Draw arrows to **match** each description to the correct character. The first has been done for you.

Diana and Mary Rivers

- feel(s) strong affection for family members
- lose(s) interest in a man when it is suggested he has no money
- discuss(es) books and learning
- accept(s) gracefully the loss of an expected inheritance
- treat(s) governesses and tutors with contempt
- care(s) for and respect(s) a lowly beggar
- treat(s) a parent with disdain
- act(s) loudly and dominate(s) the company
- admire(s) a woman for her work as a school teacher and governess

Blanche Ingram

2 Write **at least one sentence** to explain how Charlotte Brontë uses **Blanche Ingram** in the following ways:

a) As a contrast to Jane

....

....

b) As a plot device putting a problem in the way of Jane's happiness

....

....

c) To develop the theme of social status

....

....

3 Write a **paragraph** explaining whether, **in your own judgement**, Diana and Mary get what they deserve as characters at the end of the novel.

....

....

....

....

....

....

....

Practice task

1 First, **read** this **exam-style** task:

Mr Rochester has asked Jane to join him in the dining room and talk to him while Adèle unwraps her presents.

Reread from: *'Mr Rochester, as he sat in his damask-covered chair'* (Ch. 14, p. 153) to *'any other man?'* (p. 154).

Question: How does Charlotte Brontë present the relationship between Jane and Rochester in this extract?

2 Begin by circling the **key words** in the **question** above.

3 Now complete the table, noting down **three or four key points** with **evidence** and the **effect** created.

Point	Evidence/quotation	Effect or explanation

4 **Draft your response**. Use the space below for your first paragraph(s) and then continue onto a sheet of paper.

Start: *In this extract, Charlotte Brontë shows their relationship in its early stages. She suggests that Jane and Rochester are attracted to each other by ...*

....

....

....

....

....

....

PROGRESS LOG [tick the correct box]   Needs more work ☐   Getting there ☐   Under control ☐

Themes

QUICK TEST

1 **Circle** the **themes** you think are most relevant to *Jane Eyre*:

religion	families	envy	hope	the supernatural	journeys	ambition

love and marriage   greed and selfishness   female independence   social status

education   secrets and truths   justice   childhood   power   conflict

2 **Who says**? Each of these quotations relates to a theme, but which theme (or themes), and who is speaking?

a) 'I mean now to open a second school for girls.'

Theme(s): ....

Speaker: ....

b) 'Gentlemen in his station are not accustomed to marry their governesses.'

Theme(s): ....

Speaker: ....

c) 'women feel just as men feel; they need exercise for their faculties, and a field for their efforts as much as their brothers do'

Theme(s): ....

Speaker: ....

d) 'I believe; I have faith: I am going to God.'

Theme(s): ....

Speaker: ....

e) 'I will at least choose – *her I love best*. Jane, will you marry me?'

Theme(s): ....

Speaker: ....

f) 'Deceit is, indeed, a sad fault in a child'

Theme(s): ....

Speaker: ....

PROGRESS LOG [tick the correct box]   Needs more work ☐   Getting there ☐   Under control ☐

THINKING MORE DEEPLY

3 Think about the **theme** of **female independence**. Write **two or three sentences** in response to each of these questions:

a) How does Charlotte Brontë present Miss Temple and Diana and Mary Rivers?

....

....

....

....

b) How are they used to develop ideas about female independence?

....

....

....

....

4 Choose **three characters** who express strong **religious beliefs**, and summarise their attitudes in **one sentence** each:

a) ....

....

b) ....

....

c) ....

....

5 Explain in **one sentence** each how Charlotte Brontë develops the theme of **education** through these characters:

a) John Reed

....

....

b) Miss Temple

....

....

c) Adèle Varens

....

....

....

PROGRESS LOG [tick the correct box]   Needs more work ☐   Getting there ☐   Under control ☐

6 Complete this **gap-fill paragraph** about the **theme** of **love and marriage** with the correct or suitable information:

Charlotte Brontë uses the story to explore ideas about love and marriage through Jane's experiences and observations. The novel suggests that a .... marriage is based on .... The man and woman should have shared .... and feel .... to each other. Charlotte Brontë uses .... to show that marriage in her day was often based on .... and social status rather than real affection. Jane almost agrees to marry .... out of a sense of ...., but is stopped from doing so when she hears Rochester's call. Charlotte Brontë implies that Rochester finally .... Jane after repenting his errors and being humbled by .... and the loss of his hand.

7 **Think** about the **theme** of **social status**. Using **your own judgement** place these characters on each of the following status lines, using the letters a–f to represent the characters.

a) Mrs Reed

d) Mr Brocklehurst

b) Mr Rochester

e) Miss Temple

c) Mrs Fairfax

f) Diana Rivers

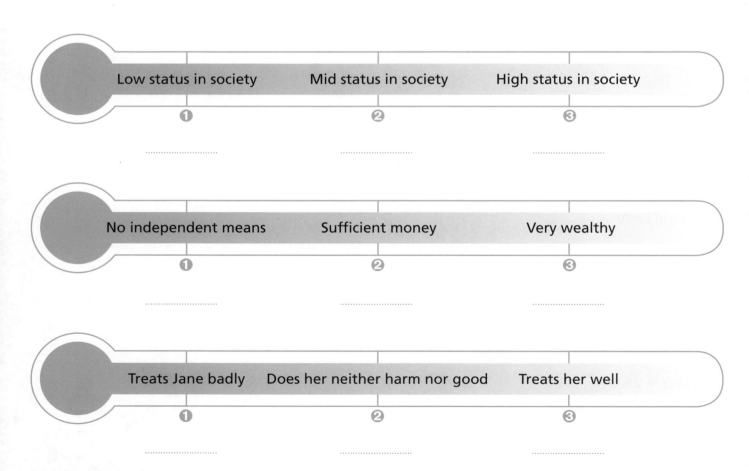

8 Now, on a separate piece of paper, write a **paragraph** explaining what the novel shows about **goodness** and **social status**.

EXAM PREPARATION: WRITING ABOUT EQUALITY

Reread the conversation between Jane and Rochester from *'Again as he kissed me'* (Ch. 37, p. 512) to *'God bless you and reward you!'* (p. 513).

Question: How does Charlotte Brontë suggest that by the time of their eventual marriage Jane and Rochester are more equal?

Think about:

- How this passage shows them as more equal than before
- How the idea of their equal status is explored in the rest of the novel

9 Complete this table:

Point/detail	Evidence	Effect or explanation
1: *Rochester feels humbled by his physical condition and grateful to Jane.*	*'I am no better than the old lightning-struck chestnut-tree'*	*Rochester's reference to the chestnut-tree shows how he has fallen from a position of pride to one of humility.*
2: *Jane still loves and values him in spite of his condition.*		
3: *We are reminded of Jane's position on marriage from Chapter 24.*		

10 Write up **point 1** into a **paragraph** below in your own words. Remember to include what you infer from the evidence, or the writer's effects.

....

....

....

....

....

11 Now, choose **one** of your **other points** and write it out as another **paragraph** here:

....

....

....

....

....

PROGRESS LOG [tick the correct box]   Needs more work ☐   Getting there ☐   Under control ☐

Contexts

QUICK TEST ✔

1 **Tick** the box for the correct answer to each of these questions:

a) From where did Charlotte Brontë get her knowledge of schools on which to base Lowood?

stories from the library ☐   a school in the village where she lived ☐

her own experience at Cowan Bridge ☐

b) Why was the role of governess important in the nineteenth century?

There were few private schools for girls ☐   Governesses were cheaper than schools ☐

Governesses were safer than schools ☐

c) What was the usual status of a governess in the household?

like a member of the family ☐   little more than a servant ☐

influential and respected ☐

d) Which genre of literature influenced Charlotte Brontë with its melodrama, haunted buildings, secrets and death?

mystery and adventure ☐   Gothic ☐   pastoral ☐

e) Which characters does Charlotte Brontë use to represent different aspects of Christianity in the novel?

Mr Brocklehurst, Helen Burns and St John ☐   John Reed and Georgiana ☐

Mrs Fairfax and Adèle Varens ☐

f) Which character(s) represent the widespread practice of marrying for wealth?

Diana and Mary Rivers ☐   Bertha and Blanche Ingram ☐

Rosamund Oliver ☐

g) What pseudonym did Charlotte Brontë use when the novel was first published?

Emily Brontë ☐   George Eliot ☐   Currer Bell ☐

THINKING MORE DEEPLY ?

2 Write **one or two sentences** in answer to each of these questions:

a) What does the novel suggest about how charitable institutions treated the people they were supposed to help?

....

....

....

....

b) Why are other characters shocked by Jane's forthright views and ability to stand up for herself?

....

....

....

....

....

c) What does the story of Celine Varens show about the treatment of women in fashionable Victorian society?

....

....

....

....

....

3 Jane expresses **strong or unconventional opinions** at several points in the story. Complete the table below with **details of what she says** to each of the characters at the time specified.

Tip: to test your knowledge, try making notes about what Jane says from memory before you check the text and complete the table.

Character	When	What Jane says
Mrs Reed	After Mr Brocklehurst has agreed to Jane going to Lockwood (Ch. 4, p. 44)	
Helen Burns	When Helen has been punished by a teacher (Ch. 6, p. 66)	
Mr Rochester	Just before he proposes to her (Ch. 23, p. 292)	
St John Rivers	When he has asked her to join him in India as his wife (Ch. 34, p. 467)	

PROGRESS LOG [tick the correct box]   Needs more work ☐   Getting there ☐   Under control ☐

Settings

1 Look at the illustrations below. Complete the name of each location, and then underneath write down **two key events** that take place there.

Gateshead ....

Events: ....

....

....

.... School

Events: ....

....

....

.... Hall

Events: ....

....

....

.... End

Events: ....

....

....

.... Manor

Events: ....

....

....

THINKING MORE DEEPLY

2 Write **three descriptive details** that Charlotte Brontë provides for each of these
settings, and comment on the **atmosphere** she creates in each:

a) The red-room (Ch. 2, pp. 16–18)

Descriptive details:

1: ....

2: ....

3: ....

Comment on the atmosphere: ....

....

b) Thornfield Hall (Ch. 11, pp. 123–25)

Descriptive details:

1: ....

2: ....

3: ....

Comment on the atmosphere: ....

....

c) Ferndean Manor (Ch. 37, pp. 496–97)

Descriptive details:

1: ....

2: ....

3: ....

Comment on the atmosphere: ....

....

3 Jane's journey from Thornfield to Marsh End is very different from her return
after hearing Rochester's call. Complete the table to compare the two:

	Leaving Thornfield (Ch. 27, pp. 368–70)	Returning to Thornfield (Ch. 36, pp. 487–88)
Jane's mood		
Imagery she uses to describe herself		
Sense of what will follow		

PROGRESS LOG [tick the correct box]   Needs more work ☐   Getting there ☐   Under control ☐

Practice task

1 First **read** this **exam-style** task:

> Mr Rochester calls Jane to help him in the middle of the night when Mason is attacked.
>
> Reread from *'Hold the candle'* (Ch. 20, p. 242) to *'the thought of Grace Poole bursting out upon me'* (p. 243).
>
> Question: Starting with this passage, explore how Charlotte Brontë uses settings to build tension. Refer closely to the passage in your answer, and then write about how settings help to build tension in the rest of the novel.

2 Begin by circling the **key words** in the **question** above.

3 Now complete the table, noting down **three or four key points** with **evidence** and the **effect** created.

Point	Evidence/quotation	Effect or explanation

4 **Draft your response.** Use the space below for your first paragraph(s) and then continue onto a sheet of paper.

Start: *In this extract, Charlotte Brontë depicts a Gothic setting that creates tension. Firstly, she ...*

....

....

....

....

....

....

....

....

PROGRESS LOG [tick the correct box]   Needs more work ☐   Getting there ☐   Under control ☐

PART FIVE: FORM, STRUCTURE AND LANGUAGE

Form

QUICK TEST ✓

1 **Tick the box** to indicate the correct word or phrase to complete each statement:

a) The novel is an example of

drama ☐   poetry ☐   prose fiction ☐

b) Charlotte Brontë has organised the novel

chronologically ☐   confusedly ☐   episodically ☐

c) A story that follows the journey of a child from naïve innocence to maturity is sometimes given the German name

Bildungsroman ☐   fable ☐   parable ☐

THINKING MORE DEEPLY ?

2 Write **two or three sentences** to describe how *Jane Eyre* fits into the **Gothic fiction** genre.

....

....

....

....

....

3 Write **one or two sentences** on each of these aspects of the novel to explain how Charlotte Brontë takes a **Romantic** approach to them:

a) The weather

....

....

b) The voice of the 'common man' or ordinary person

....

....

c) Characters' emotions

....

....

....

PROGRESS LOG [tick the correct box]   Needs more work ☐   Getting there ☐   Under control ☐

Structure

QUICK TEST

1 The stages of Jane's journey through life are represented by the **five main locations** in the novel. **Number** these locations so that they are in the **correct sequence** in which they first appear in the novel. Use 1 for the first location and 5 for the final location:

a) Thornfield Hall ☐ d) Ferndean Manor ☐

b) Gateshead Hall ☐ e) Lowood School ☐

c) Marsh End / Moor House ☐

THINKING MORE DEEPLY

2 How does Charlotte Brontë use **journeys** as an important structural feature in the novel? Complete this table about two of the journeys that Jane makes:

	How she travels	How Jane's character is developed
From Gateshead to Lowood School (Chapter 5)		
From Thornfield to Marsh End (Chapter 28)		

3 **Complete these quotations** which show that Jane is telling her story from the perspective of looking back ten years after her arrival at Ferndean:

a) 'now, at the distance of – I will not say how many .... – I see it clearly.'

b) 'Such was the characteristic of Helen's discourse on that, to me, ... evening'

c) 'But what is so .... as youth'

d) 'Gentle reader, may you never feel what I .... felt!'

e) 'Some say there is enjoyment in looking back to painful experience past; but at this day I can scarcely bear to .... the times to which I allude'

f) 'one brief glance at the fortunes of those whose names have most frequently recurred in this ...., and I have done.'

Reread the description of Jane's first journey to Thornfield at the start of Chapter 11 from the opening of the chapter (p. 111) to *'I alighted and went in'* (p. 113).

Question: How does Charlotte Brontë use this passage to create an impression of a new phase in Jane's life?

Think about:

- Jane's thoughts and emotions
- The imagery Charlotte Brontë uses

Complete this table:

Point/detail	Evidence	Effect or explanation
1: *The narrator points out the significance of this journey.*	*She uses the metaphors of a 'new chapter' and a 'new scene in a play'.*	*Charlotte Brontë shows that the narrator is shaping her 'autobiography' and creating anticipation as to what will follow.*
2: *Jane has mixed feelings.*		
3: *The weather helps to build tension.*		

❺ Write up point 1 in a **paragraph** below, in your own words. Remember to include what you infer from the evidence or the writer's effects:

....

....

....

....

❻ Now, choose **one** of your **other points** and write it out as another **paragraph** here:

....

....

....

....

....

PROGRESS LOG [tick the correct box]   Needs more work ☐   Getting there ☐   Under control ☐

Language

QUICK TEST ✔

1 Which of these statements about the novel are **TRUE** and which are **FALSE**? Write **'T'** or **'F'** in the boxes:

a) The novel is written in the third person. ☐

b) A non-fiction account of a life told by the subject is called an autobiography. ☐

c) Jane never addresses the reader directly. ☐

d) Charlotte Brontë uses imagery from the natural world to suggest particular meanings. ☐

e) Charlotte Brontë uses dreams as important symbols for Jane's interior life. ☐

f) There is no significance to the names that Charlotte Brontë gives her characters. ☐

g) The narrative is written entirely in the past tense. ☐

THINKING MORE DEEPLY ?

2 Write **two or three sentences** to explain how Charlotte Brontë has used imagery to convey ideas about characters in each of these quotations:

a) Blanche Ingram: 'her mind was poor, her heart barren by nature: nothing bloomed spontaneously on that soil; no unforced natural fruit delighted by its freshness' **(Ch. 18, pp. 215–16)**

....

....

....

....

....

....

b) St John Rivers: 'came in out of the frozen hurricane … the cloak that covered his tall figure all white as a glacier' **(Ch. 33, p. 435)**

....

....

....

....

....

....

THINKING MORE DEEPLY

c) **Jane described by Rochester:** 'the soul made of fire, and the character that bends but does not break … I like the sense of pliancy you impart; and while I am twining the soft, silken skein round my finger, it sends a thrill up my arm to my heart' **(Ch. 24, pp. 300–01)**

....

....

....

....

....

....

d) **Mr Rochester:** 'his presence in a room was more cheering than the brightest fire' **(Ch. 15, p. 172)**

....

....

....

....

....

....

3 **Complete** this table to explore how Charlotte Brontë uses **Gothic imagery**:

	Examples of Gothic imagery	Effect or explanation
Jane's thoughts in the red-room (Ch. 2, pp. 20–21)	*'the dimly gleaming mirror'* *'dead men … revisiting the earth'* *A sudden mysterious light* *Jane's physical sensations of horror*	*Charlotte Brontë builds tension through Jane's fears and imaginings in the dark, gloomy room. Her intense expression of emotion makes her appear all the more vulnerable.*
The night of the fire in Rochester's room (Ch. 15, p. 173)		
Thornfield Hall on Jane's return (Ch. 36, pp. 489–90)		

PROGRESS LOG [tick the correct box]   Needs more work ☐   Getting there ☐   Under control ☐

EXAM PREPARATION: WRITING ABOUT LANGUAGE

Question: How does Charlotte Brontë use language which describes the natural world to convey ideas related to events and characters?

Think about:

- The use of pathetic fallacy
- The different moods created by different natural scenes

4 Complete this table:

Point/detail	Evidence	Effect or explanation
1: *Charlotte Brontë uses personification to present the natural world.*	*'a kindly star'* *'the moon shut herself wholly within her chamber'*	*This reflects the Romantic fallacy that nature can feel human emotions. It makes Charlotte Brontë's description more vivid.*
2: *Nature seems to share or react to characters' emotions.*		
3: *Charlotte Brontë describes nature at significant moments in the story.*		

5 Write up **point 1** in a **paragraph** below in your own words. Remember to include what you infer from the evidence, or the writer's effects:

....

....

....

....

....

....

6 Now, choose **one** of your **other points** and write it out as another **paragraph** here:

....

....

....

....

....

....

....

PROGRESS LOG [tick the correct box]   Needs more work ☐   Getting there ☐   Under control ☐

Practice task

1 First, **read** this **exam-style** task:

On the day before her wedding, Jane is waiting for Rochester to return to Thornfield.

Reread from: *'I sought the orchard'* (Ch. 25, p. 318) to *'I ran off again'* (p. 319).

Question: How does Charlotte Brontë use nature imagery to convey Jane's character and situation in this extract and at other times in the novel?

Think about:

● The imagery used to describe nature
● Jane's emotions and what happens to her next

2 Begin by circling the **key words** in the **question** above.

3 Now complete the table, noting down **three or four key points** with **evidence** and the **effect** created:

Point	Evidence/quotation	Effect or explanation

4 **Draft your response**. Use the space below for your first paragraph(s) and then continue onto a sheet of paper.

Start: *In this extract, Charlotte Brontë uses nature to create a sense of foreboding as Jane waits to tell Rochester about what happened the night before. Firstly, …*

....

....

....

....

....

PROGRESS LOG [tick the correct box]   Needs more work ☐   Getting there ☐   Under control ☐

PART SIX: Progress Booster

Expressing and explaining ideas

1 How well can you express your ideas about *Jane Eyre*? Look at this grid and tick the level you think you are currently at:

Level	How you respond	Writing skills	Tick
High	• You analyse the effect of specific words and phrases very closely (i.e. 'zooming in' on them and exploring their meaning). • You select quotations very carefully and you embed them fluently in your sentences. • You are persuasive and convincing in the points you make, often coming up with original ideas.	You use a wide range of specialist terms (words like 'imagery'), excellent punctuation, accurate spelling, grammar, etc.	
Mid/Good	• You analyse some parts of the text closely, but not all the time. • You support what you say with evidence and quotations, but sometimes your writing could be more fluent to read. • You make relevant comments on the text.	You use a good range of specialist terms, generally accurate punctuation, usually accurate spelling, grammar, etc.	
Lower	• You comment on some words and phrases but often you do not develop your ideas. • You sometimes use quotations to back up what you say but they are not always well chosen. • You mention the effect of certain words and phrases but these are not always relevant to the task.	You do not have a very wide range of specialist terms, but you have reasonably accurate spelling, punctuation and grammar.	

SELECTING AND USING QUOTATIONS

2 Read these two samples from students' responses to a question about how Blanche Ingram is presented. Decide which of the three levels they fit best, i.e. **lower** (L), **mid** (M) or **high** (H).

Student A: *Blanche is insensitive to Jane when she talks about governesses. She continues her criticisms 'still loud enough for me to hear' even though Jane is present. It shows us that Blanche is mean and strong-minded.*

Level? ☐ Why? ....

....

Student B: *Charlotte Brontë demonstrates Blanche's insensitivity and arrogance when she continues to voice her criticism of governesses 'still loud enough' for Jane to hear, even after Mrs Dent reminds her of Jane's presence. Blanche's self-confidence and unwillingness to be guided by others make her an unattractive character and elicit the reader's sympathy for Jane.*

Level? ☐ Why? ....

....

*AO4 is assessed by OCR only.

ZOOMING IN – YOUR TURN!

Here is the first part of another student response. The student has picked a good quotation but hasn't 'zoomed in' on any particular words or phrases:

As Blanche entertains the group with stories of how she treated her governesses, she describes Miss Wilson, as 'not worth the trouble of vanquishing', revealing her contempt for other people.

3 Pick out one of the **words** or **phrases** the student has quoted and write a further sentence to complete the explanation:

The word/phrase '...' suggests that ....

....

....

EXPLAINING IDEAS

You need to be precise about the way Charlotte Brontë gets ideas across. This can be done by varying your use of verbs (not just using 'says' or 'means').

4 Read this paragraph from a **mid-level** response to a question about Blanche's relationship with Rochester. Circle all the **verbs** that are repeated (not in the quotations):

The novel shows us that Blanche is not suited to Rochester when Jane says she 'could not charm him'. It not only says there is little attraction between the two in spite of Blanche's efforts, but also shows that Jane is astute enough to understand better than Blanche what is going on.

5 Now choose some of the words below to replace your circled ones:

suggests	implies	tells us	presents	signals	asks	indicates
demonstrates	recognises	comprehends	reveals	conveys		

6 Rewrite your **high-level** version of the paragraph in full below. Remember to mention the **author by name** to show you understand she is **making choices** in how she presents characters, themes and events.

....

....

....

....

....

....

....

....

PROGRESS LOG [tick the correct box]   Needs more work ☐   Getting there ☐   Under control ☐

Making inferences and interpretations

WRITING ABOUT INFERENCES

You need to be able to show you can read between the lines, and make inferences, rather than just explain more explicit 'surface' meanings.

Here is an extract from one student's **high-level** response to a question about Miss Temple and how she is presented:

In Chapter 7, Miss Temple shows her disapproval of Mr Brocklehurst and his views about how the school should be run when she 'gazed straight before her' with an expression of 'petrified severity'. This tells us that although her position in the school means she has to listen to him politely, her views are unchanged by what he says. Charlotte Brontë uses the dialogue between the two characters to convey Miss Temple's excellent principles in comparison with Mr Brocklehurst's absurdity and hypocrisy.

1 Look at the response carefully.

- **Underline** the simple point which explains what Miss Temple does.
- **Circle** the sentence that develops the first point.
- **Highlight** the sentence that shows an inference and begins to explore wider interpretations.

INTERPRETING – YOUR TURN!

2 Read the opening to this student response carefully and then **choose the concluding phrase** from the list below which shows **inference** and could lead to **a deeper interpretation**. Remember – interpreting is *not* guesswork!

Even on her deathbed, Mrs Reed finds it hard to admit that she was at fault in her treatment of Jane when she murmurs to herself, 'I may get better, and to humble myself so to her is painful.' This shows that she is still a very proud woman. It also suggests that …

a) *she admires and respects Jane now.*

b) *she is telling the truth now only to clear her conscience in preparation for meeting God after death.*

c) *she feels that she might recover and doesn't like the idea of having to face Jane.*

3 Now **complete** this **paragraph** about St John Rivers, adding your own final sentence which makes inferences or explores wider interpretations:

St John is presented as an austere, inflexible Christian by Charlotte Brontë, and as someone who sacrifices personal happiness for his faith. At the end, Jane reports that, 'his glorious sun hastens to its setting.' This suggests that ....

....

....

PROGRESS LOG [tick the correct box]   Needs more work ☐   Getting there ☐   Under control ☐

Writing about context

EXPLAINING CONTEXT

When you write about context you must make sure that what you write is relevant to the task.

Read this comment by a student about Jane:

The situation of women in nineteenth-century society is reflected partly by Jane's thoughts on marriage in the novel. She is pleased to receive her inheritance from her uncle, John Eyre because it gives her the opportunity either to live independently as a single woman or to choose a husband for love and compatibility rather than as a 'mere money speculation'.

1 Why is this an effective paragraph about context? Select a), b) or c).

a) Because it explains how important money is to Jane.

b) Because it makes the link between the position of women at the time and Jane's character.

c) Because it tells us about inheritances in the nineteenth century.

YOUR TURN!

2 Now read this further paragraph, and complete it by choosing a suitable point related to context, selecting from a), b) or c) below.

Charlotte Brontë makes characters' attitudes to marriage a key feature of the novel, and she uses them to mirror elements of society at the time. Marriage was often seen as a means of gaining financial security or growing the family fortune rather than as the fulfilment of true love. This can be seen in Rochester's words when he says …

a) *'You are my sympathy – my better self – my good angel'. This shows that married people should influence each other for good.*

b) *'was not sure of the existence of one virtue in her nature', which shows that he hardly knew Bertha when he married her.*

c) *'I must be provided for by a wealthy marriage', which shows that his father's actions in arranging the match with Bertha were motivated by money.*

3 Now, on a separate sheet of paper, write a paragraph about how Charlotte Brontë uses the context of charitable institutions for orphans in the nineteenth century to present Jane's experience at Lowood School (for example, how the girls are treated).

PROGRESS LOG [tick the correct box]   Needs more work ☐   Getting there ☐   Under control ☐

Structure and linking of paragraphs

Paragraphs need to demonstrate your points clearly by:

- Using topic sentences
- Focusing on key words from quotations
- Explaining their effect or meaning

1 Read this model paragraph in which a student explains how Charlotte Brontë presents Jane.

Charlotte Brontë presents Jane as someone who makes her own judgements. She expresses her opinions of the teachers at Lowood to Helen Burns but finds they disagree: 'Still less could I understand or sympathise with the forbearance she expressed'. The word 'forbearance' reflects Helen's Christian principles of acceptance, but Jane prefers standing up for justice instead of suffering passively.

Look at the response carefully.

- **Underline** the topic sentence which explains the main point about Jane.
- **Circle** the word that is picked out from the quotation.
- **Highlight** or put a tick next to the part of the last sentence which explains the word.

2 Now read this paragraph by a student who is explaining how Charlotte Brontë presents John Reed and his relationship with Jane:

We find out about John Reed when Jane says 'every nerve I had feared him, and every morsel of flesh on my bones shrank when he came near.' This tells us that she is afraid of him.

Expert viewpoint: This paragraph is unclear. It does not begin with a topic sentence to explain how Charlotte Brontë presents Jane's relationship with John Reed and doesn't zoom in on any key words that tell us what the relationship is like.

Now **rewrite the paragraph**. Start with a **topic sentence**, and pick out a **key word or phrase** to **'zoom in'** on, then follow up with an explanation or interpretation.

Charlotte Brontë presents John Reed as someone who Jane ....

....

....

....

....

....

....

....

....

....

....

It is equally important to make your sentences link together and your ideas follow on fluently from each other. You can do this by:

- Using a mixture of short and long sentences as appropriate
- Using words or phrases that help connect or develop ideas

3 Read this model paragraph by one student writing about Diana Rivers and how she is presented:

Charlotte Brontë presents Diana as a strong, independent woman who is a role model for Jane. She contributes to the theme of independence by earning her living as a governess, even though she dislikes the family for whom she works. A 'balm-like' presence surrounds Jane when Diana feeds her, and Jane admires her learning and abilities as a teacher. At the end of the novel Charlotte Brontë rewards Diana's goodness. We are told that she has married for love to a 'good man', implying that, like Jane, she has found the happiness she deserves.

Look at the response carefully.

- **Underline** the topic sentence which introduces the main idea.
- **Underline** the short sentence which signals a change in ideas.
- **Circle** any words or phrases that link ideas such as 'who', 'when', 'implying', 'which', etc.

4 Read this paragraph by another student commenting on how Bertha Rochester is presented:

Charlotte Brontë gives us a vivid picture of Bertha Rochester. This is in the description of her after the wedding in Chapter 26. She says it is not clear whether Bertha is 'beast or human'. This gives the impression that she is wild and dangerous. It suggests someone inhuman. She also makes animal noises. The description also says she moves on all fours.

> **Expert viewpoint:** The candidate has understood how the character's nature is revealed in her appearance. However, the paragraph is rather awkwardly written. It needs improving by linking the sentences with suitable phrases and joining words such as: 'where', 'in', 'as well as', 'who', 'suggesting', 'implying'.

Rewrite the **paragraph**, improving the **style**, and also try to add a **concluding sentence** on how Bertha is presented.

Start with the same **topic sentence**, but extend it:

Charlotte Brontë gives us a vivid picture of Bertha Rochester ....

....

....

....

....

....

....

....

PROGRESS LOG [tick the correct box]   Needs more work ☐   Getting there ☐   Under control ☐

Writing skills

Here are a number of key words you might use when writing in the exam:

Content and structure	Characters and style	Linguistic features
chapter	character	metaphor
scene	role	personification
quotation	protagonist	juxtaposition
sequence	dramatic	dramatic irony
dialogue	tragedy	repetition
climax	narrator	symbol
development	humorous	foreshadowing
description	sympathetic	euphemism

1 Circle any you might find difficult to spell, and then use the 'Look, Say, Cover, Write, Check' method to learn them. This means: **look** at the word; **say** it out loud; then **cover** it up; **write** it out; uncover and **check** your spelling with the correct version.

2 Create a **mnemonic** for five of your difficult spellings. For example:

tragedy: **t**en **r**eally **a**ngry **g**irls **e**njoyed **d**ancing **y**esterday! Or …

break the word down: T – RAGE – DY!

a) ....

b) ....

c) ....

d) ....

e) ....

3 Circle any **incorrect spellings** in this paragraph and then rewrite it:

Brontie uses jurneys as structurl devises marking the shifts between stages of Jane's life. Her experiense of travel reflects Jane's emotions; for example, her lonelyness is symbolysed by the empty coach that drives her away from Thornfeild. The 'place a long way off' is a metaphore which implys that her future is uncertain.

....

....

....

....

....

....

....

*AO4 is assessed by OCR only.

4 **Punctuation** can help make your meaning clear.

Here is one response by a student commenting on Charlotte Brontë's choice of the name 'Temple' for Jane's much-admired teacher. Check for correct use of:

- Apostrophes
- Speech marks for quotations and emphasis
- Full stops, commas and capital letters

When Charlotte Brontë gives the Lowood superintendent the name of 'Temple', we think of holy places which are associated with goodness, and spiritual growth this is an apt choice because Miss Temple is a person full of goodness' who has strong principles She sets an excellent example, to the girls' in her care.

Rewrite it **correctly** here:

....

....

....

....

....

....

5 It is better to use the **present tense** to describe what is happening in the novel.

Look at these two extracts. Which one uses tenses **consistently** and **accurately**?

Student A: *Charlotte Brontë told us through Jane's conversation with Diana that St John Rivers 'will never forgive' her for rejecting him, and so emphasised the strength of his will. His attitude is opposite to that of Rochester who felt 'blessed' even to have her back as a friend.*

Student B: *Charlotte Brontë tells us through Jane's conversation with Diana that St John Rivers 'will never forgive' her for rejecting him, and so emphasises the strength of his will. His attitude is opposite to that of Rochester who feels 'blessed' even to have her back as a friend.*

6 Now look at this further paragraph. **Underline** or **circle** all the verb **tenses** first.

Mrs Fairfax tried to make Jane see that she was at risk of being seduced by Rochester and wants to put Jane on her guard. She warned Jane that 'all is not gold that glitters'. This proverb was an image Charlotte Brontë used to imply that Jane was tempted by Rochester's wealth.

Now rewrite it using the **present tense** consistently:

....

....

....

....

....

....

PROGRESS LOG [tick the correct box]   Needs more work ☐   Getting there ☐   Under control ☐

Tackling exam tasks

DECODING QUESTIONS

It is important to be able to identify key words in exam tasks and then quickly generate some ideas.

1 Read this task and notice how the **key words** have been underlined.

Question: *In what ways does <u>Rochester respond</u> to <u>Jane throughout the novel</u>?*

Write about:

- How Rochester responds to Jane both <u>at the start</u> of their relationship, and as the <u>novel progresses</u>
- How Charlotte Brontë <u>presents Rochester</u> by the <u>way she writes</u>

Now do the same with this task, i.e. underline the key words:

Question: *Explain how Charlotte Brontë explores ideas about social status in the novel.*

Write about:

- Ideas about social status and wealth
- How Charlotte Brontë presents those ideas

GENERATING IDEAS

2 Now you need to generate ideas quickly in response to the question above. Use the spider diagram* below and add as many ideas of your own as you can:

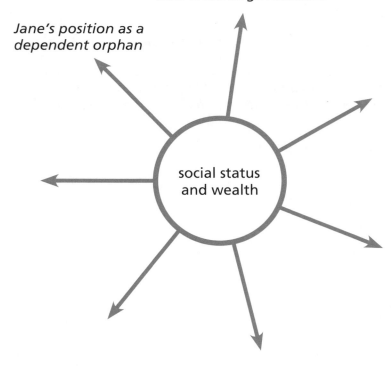

The position of women who work as governesses

Jane's position as a dependent orphan

social status and wealth

*You can do this as a list if you wish.

PLANNING AN ESSAY

Here is the **exam-style** task from the previous page:

Question: *Explain how Charlotte Brontë explores ideas about social status in the novel.*

Write about:

- Ideas about status and wealth in society
- How Charlotte Brontë presents those ideas

3 **Using the ideas you generated,** write a simple **plan** with at least **five key points** (the first two have been done for you). Check back to your spider diagram or the list you made.

a) *The Reed family's treatment of Jane – due to her low status as dependent orphan*

b) *The position of respectable women who have to work as governesses*

c) ....

d) ....

e) ....

4 Now list **five quotations**, one for each point (the first two have been provided for you):

a) *John Reed says to Jane: 'you have no money … you ought to beg, and not live here with gentlemen's children like us … at our mamma's expense'.*

b) *Blanche refers to governesses as 'the whole tribe' and says 'they are a nuisance'.*

c) ....
....

d) ....
....

e) ....
....

5 Now read this task and **write a plan of your own**, including **quotations**, on a separate sheet of paper.

Reread from *'The post-chaise stopped; the driver rang the door-bell'* (Ch. 18, p. 220) to *'and such a placid eye and smile!'* (p. 221).

Question: *How is Richard Mason depicted in this extract, and how does Jane regard him?*

PROGRESS LOG [tick the correct box]   Needs more work ☐   Getting there ☐   Under control ☐

Sample answers

OPENING PARAGRAPHS

Here is the task from the previous page:

Question: *Explain how Charlotte Brontë explores ideas about social status in the novel.*

Now look at these two alternate openings to the essay and read the examiner comments underneath:

Student A

> *Charlotte Brontë explores ideas about social status through Jane's experiences with different characters and her thoughts about them. The Reeds look down on Jane, treating her badly because she is poor. Later, Blanche Ingram shows off by speaking contemptuously of governesses when Jane is present. But Jane is not intimidated because she believes that people can be equal however different their wealth, age or importance.*

Student B

> *Some characters treat Jane badly because she is poor. The Reeds bully her. Blanche Ingram is very snobbish. She looks down on Jane because she is only a governess who works for the family, and Blanche wants to marry Mr Rochester because he is rich.*

Expert viewpoint 1: This is a clear opening paragraph that outlines some of the details to be discussed. It also covers different parts of the novel and links the theme to Jane's character and values. It could also have mentioned how institutions such as Lowood School reflect ideas about social status.

Expert viewpoint 2: This opening recounts characters' actions and relationships without outlining what is to be discussed in the essay, which is the point of an introduction. It should have referred to the author and used words linked to the question on social status.

❶ Which comment belongs to which answer? Match the paragraph (A or B) to the expert's feedback (1 or 2).

Student A: ....   **Student B:** ....

❷ Now it's your turn. Write the opening paragraph to this task on a separate sheet of paper:

Reread from *'The post-chaise stopped; the driver rang the door-bell'* (Ch. 18, p. 220) to *'and such a placid eye and smile!'* (p. 221).

Question: *How is Richard Mason depicted in this extract, and how does Jane regard him?*

Remember:

● Introduce the topic in general terms, perhaps **explaining** or **'unpicking'** the key **words** or **ideas** in the task (such as 'depicted').

● Mention the **different possibilities** or ideas that you are going to address.

● Use the **author's name**.

*AO4 is assessed by OCR only.

WRITING ABOUT TECHNIQUES

Here are two paragraphs in response to a different task, where the students have focused on the writer's techniques. The task is:

Reread from: '*Meantime, Mr Brocklehurst, standing on the hearth*' (Ch. 7, p. 75) to '*she wore a false front of French curls.*' (p. 77).

Question: *What techniques does Charlotte Brontë use to imply criticism of Mr Brocklehurst in this extract?*

Student A

> *Miss Temple passes her handkerchief over her lips to hide a smile. This tells us that she thinks his behaviour is ridiculous even though he is a clergyman with authority at Lowood. The way Charlotte Brontë shows other characters in relation to Brocklehurst drives home her message to the reader about him. And we know that he is later criticised and removed from his position.*

Student B

> *Charlotte Brontë has already established Miss Temple as a wise, sympathetic character, so when she 'passed her handkerchief over her lips' to hide her smile Charlotte Brontë is ridiculing Brocklehurst's behaviour. Charlotte Brontë also uses irony to show Brocklehurst's hypocrisy when his wife and daughters arrive wearing fashionable, rich clothes immediately after his lecture on the dangers of vanity. This shows Charlotte Brontë's disapproval of Brocklehurst and the religious values that he represents, a theme that she develops throughout the novel.*

Expert viewpoint 1: This high-level response clearly states the effect on the reader of Charlotte Brontë's writing. It uses literary terms effectively to show understanding of the techniques she uses. It gives an interpretative response using abstract nouns to good effect. The final sentence links to the wider theme, though it could have been more precise about Brocklehurst's religious beliefs.

Expert viewpoint 2: This mid-level response highlights Miss Temple's response to Brocklehurst. However, it does not give enough detail about how Charlotte Brontë uses other characters to criticise him. It does not focus enough on the writer's technique, and the point about Charlotte Brontë's criticism of him is not sufficiently developed.

❸ Which comment belongs to which answer? Match the paragraph (A or B) to the expert's feedback (1 or 2).

Student A: ....   **Student B:** ....

❹ Now, take another **aspect** of the extract and on a separate sheet of paper write your own **paragraph**. You could **comment** on one of these aspects:

- Mr Brocklehurst's pompous language
- How the girls of the school react to him
- His injustice to Jane

Read this **lower-level** response to the following task:

Reread from '*Habitually obedient to John, I came up to his chair*' (Ch. 1, p. 12) to '*you are like the Roman emperors!*' (p. 13).

Question: *How is John Reed depicted in this passage, and how does Jane respond to him?*

Student response

> When Jane stands in front of him John sits there, '*he spent some three minutes thrusting out his tongue at me*'. This means he sticks his tongue out at Jane. He also puts her down with mean comments. He is not bothered by his mum or anyone in his family because he is spoilt and they can't make him do anything.
>
> John wants Jane to be scared of him. He wants her to feel inferior so he asks questions and tells her off. He makes her stand in the corner so he can throw the book at her without her seeing.

Expert viewpoint: The quotation in paragraph one is well chosen and gives us a sense of John's treatment of Jane, but there is no attempt to embed it in a sentence. Nor is there any exploration in either paragraph of the effect that John has on Jane and how she responds. Comments on what Charlotte Brontë intends in this passage are needed. The language the student uses is sometimes too informal, as in, 'puts her down'.

⑤ Rewrite these two **paragraphs** in your own words, improving them by addressing:

- The lack of development of linking of points – no '**zooming in**' on **key words and phrases**
- The lack of **quotations and embedding**
- Unnecessary **repetition**, poor **specialist terms** and use of **vocabulary**

Paragraph 1:

In this scene, Charlotte Brontë depicts John Reed as ....

....

and also ....

....

This implies that ....

....

Paragraph 2:

Jane's response to John at first is ....

....

However, ...

....

This links to ....

....

A FULL-LENGTH RESPONSE

6 Write a **full-length response** to this exam-style task on a separate sheet of paper. Answer both parts of the question:

Question: *How does Charlotte Brontë present the character of Mr Rochester throughout the novel?*

Write about:

- How Charlotte Brontë presents him before Jane leaves Thornfield
- How Charlotte Brontë presents him when Jane returns to Ferndean Manor

Remember to do the following:

- Plan **quickly** (no more than 5 minutes) what you intend to write, jotting down **four or five supporting quotations**.
- Refer closely to the **key words** in the question.
- Make sure you comment on **what** the writer does, the **techniques** he uses and the **effect** of those techniques.
- Support your points with **well-chosen quotations** or other evidence.
- Develop your points by **'zooming in'** on particular **words** or **phrases** and explaining their **effect**.
- Be **persuasive** and **convincing** in what you say.
- Check carefully for **spelling**, **punctuation** and **grammar**.

PROGRESS LOG [tick the correct box]   Needs more work ☐   Getting there ☐   Under control ☐

Further questions

1 What message do you think Charlotte Brontë is trying to convey about religion in the novel?

2 How far do you agree that *Jane Eyre* is a Gothic novel?

3 How does Charlotte Brontë present Jane's eventual union with Rochester as a marriage of equals?

4 Journeys play an important part in the novel. How do they help to tell Jane's story?

5 There are several themes in the novel, such as equality, independence and marriage. What do you think is the most important theme and why? (You can write about a theme not mentioned.)

PROGRESS LOG [tick the correct box]   Needs more work ☐   Getting there ☐   Under control ☐

ANSWERS

NOTE: Answers have been provided for most tasks. Exceptions are 'Practice tasks' and tasks which ask you to write a paragraph or to use your own words or judgement.

PART TWO: PLOT AND ACTION

Chapter 1 [pp. 8–9]

1 a) John Reed; b) November; c) behind the curtain on a window seat; d) John throws a book at her; e) Bessie; f) by locking her in the red-room

2 a) The book, Bewick's *History of British Birds*, contains pictures of wild, cold and lonely places that mirror the bleak November weather and Jane's feeling of isolation.

   b) He is physically 'unwholesome' and spoilt by his mother. He is a bully who dominates the house because the servants are afraid of him, and his mother is 'blind and deaf' to his behaviour.

   c) The story is told in Jane's voice so we understand and sympathise with her point of view.

3

Point/detail	Evidence	Effect or explanation
1: The description of a miserably cold day creates a dismal picture of Jane's experience.	'dreadful to me was the coming home in the raw twilight, with nipped fingers and toes'	Her physical suffering seems to reflect the emotional coldness she experiences.
2: Jane feels like an outsider with the Reed children.	'humbled by the consciousness of my physical inferiority'	Jane's physical appearance shows that she isn't one of the family and her small stature makes her seem vulnerable.
3: The Reeds enjoy comfort and luxury while Jane is excluded.	'she lay reclined on a sofa … with her darlings about her … Me, she had dispensed from joining the group'	Mrs Reed favours her own children and shows no affection for Jane.

Chapters 2–3 [pp. 10–11]

1 a) 3; b) 6; c) 1; d) 4; e) 2; f) 7; g) 5

2 a) The accounts of school that Jane has heard from Bessie and John Reed make the discipline there sound appalling. But she is attracted by the idea of the things she could learn, and sees school as an escape from Gateshead.

   b) Her father, a poor clergyman, married her mother whose wealthy family disowned her. Both parents died from typhus when Jane was very young.

   c) Bessie treats Jane kindly when she is ill by bringing her food on a favourite plate and a book. She sings to her and encourages her to be more cheerful.

3

Point/detail	Evidence	Effect or explanation
1: Thinking of her dead uncle turns Jane's thoughts to spirits and ghosts.	'I began to recall what I had heard of dead men … revisiting the earth'	Charlotte Brontë increases the tension as Jane describes ghostly actions in a long, breathless sentence.
2: A mysterious light increases her sense of horror.	'a light gleamed on the wall'	Charlotte Brontë adds a visual detail to increase the sense of horror approaching.
3: Jane's fear produces strong physical effects.	'My heart beat thick, my head grew hot; a sound filled my ears … I was oppressed, suffocated'	By including these physical effects, Charlotte Brontë shows that Jane's fear is overwhelming.

Chapter 4 [pp. 12–13]

1 a) F; b) T; c) T; d) F; e) F; f) T

2 a) The first person narrative reveals that Jane has different thoughts and opinions from the adults around her. She summons up her courage to challenge Mrs Reed by stating the truth about how she has been treated.

   b) His appearance is intimidating – 'a black pillar' and a 'grim face'. Charlotte Brontë uses exclamations to show that he reminds Jane of the wolf from 'Little Red Riding Hood'.

   c) Jane knows that Bessie, unlike the other adults, doesn't mean any harm when she is angry. Bessie says she is fonder of Jane than of the others, and they enjoy an afternoon of 'peace and harmony' together.

3

Point/detail	Evidence	Effect or explanation
1: Jane speaks from a strong sense of injustice because Mrs Reed told Mr Brocklehurst she was deceitful.	'Speak I must: I had been trodden on severely, and must turn'	Jane's repetition of the word 'must' shows her conviction and the necessity to her of telling the truth.
2: Jane has the confidence to uphold what she knows is right.	'How dare I? Because it is the truth.'	The verb 'dare' expresses the boldness of Jane's behaviour. Knowing that she is morally right gives Jane the courage to act.
3: Charlotte Brontë makes the Reeds unattractive characters by showing that they are deceitful or hypocritical.	Jane says that Georgiana tells lies, and she identifies the hypocrisy in Mrs Reed's behaviour.	Charlotte Brontë creates a contrast between Jane and the others to make the reader sympathise with her.

Chapters 5–6 [pp. 14–15]

1 a) January; b) porridge; c) Miss/Maria Temple; d) Miss Scatcherd; e) Helen Burns; f) establishment/concern/institution

2 a) It is a cold and comfortless place with poor food and strict discipline, including corporal punishment. The girls' time is ruled by bells, and they have to stand for long hours during lessons.

   b) Helen follows the Bible's guidance that 'bids us return good for evil'. Jane, however, believes that she 'must resist those who punish [her] unjustly'.

   c) Miss Temple inspires admiration and awe in Jane, appearing attractive, elegant and refined. She shows compassion and courage by ordering extra food for the girls, and is described as 'full of goodness'.

3

Point/detail	Evidence	Effect or explanation
1: Jane is being sent away from everything she has known so far.	Jane describes being 'severed' from Bessie and Gateshead when the coach drives away.	Charlotte Brontë uses the word 'severed' to suggest a painful parting, and to signify the breaking of old ties.
2: She does not know what will happen in the next phase of her life.	' thus whirled away to unknown … remote and mysterious regions'	The adjectives 'remote' and 'mysterious' create a sense of Romantic anticipation of the next stage in Jane's story. She seems to welcome the prospect of new possibilities and experiences in her life that the journey opens up.
3: The unfamiliar towns and countryside give Jane an impression of great distance.	'I began to feel that we were getting very far indeed from Gateshead'	The physical change of scene is a metaphor for the change that is being made in Jane's life.

Chapters 7–8 [pp. 16–17]

1 a) 6; b) 4; c) 1; d) 2; e) 7; f) 5; g) 3

2 a) Sundays at Lowood are described as 'dreary days' on which the girls suffer even more from cold and lack of food as they attend church, learn their scripture and listen to a sermon. Religious practice at Lowood brings them no joy or any experience of Christian kindness.

b) It is ironic that Mr Brocklehurst lectures the school about the dangers of vanity, and orders that the girls with long and curled hair have it cut off when his wife and daughters are 'splendidly attired' in expensive, fashionable clothes with their hair 'elaborately curled'.

c) Jane is strengthened by Helen's support and calmed by her words. Helen makes Jane reflect on other ways of thinking, and Jane is inspired by the extent of her knowledge.

3

Point/detail	Evidence	Effect or explanation
1: The restoration of her reputation is a very important event for Jane.	'Thus relieved of a grievous load'	The metaphor 'grievous load' shows that Jane suffers the disgrace of being called a liar, and wants the people she likes to know her true moral worth.
2: With the injustices of Mrs Reed and Mr Brocklehurst behind her, Jane can now look forward in her new life.	'I from that hour set to work afresh, resolved to pioneer my way through every difficulty.'	The words 'resolved' and 'pioneer' show that Jane now boldly faces the challenges ahead. She improves in her lessons and enjoys learning.
3: Jane realises the value of love in a poor environment over hatred and unhappiness in a rich one.	'I would not now have exchanged Lowood with all its privations for Gateshead and all its daily luxuries.'	This passage establishes the personal values and a sense of priorities that will be important to Jane as her story progresses.

Chapters 9–10 [pp. 18–19]

1 a) T; b) T; c) F; d) F; e) F; f) T; g) F

2 a) By making Jane address the reader directly Charlotte Brontë conveys a realistic impression of a character telling her own story. It reminds us that Jane is telling her story looking back from the perspective of adulthood and reflecting on her childhood experiences.

b) Helen raises the subject of Christian faith and her belief that she will return to God when she dies. Jane is full of questions about where God is and what heaven means.

c) Whereas Jane has prospered through hard work to become well educated and happy, the Reed children have turned out badly. John leads a dissipated life and the girls quarrel.

3

Point/detail	Evidence	Effect or explanation
1: Charlotte Brontë makes a contrast between harsh winter and the softer spring.	'cutting winds' become 'gentler breathings'	Personification makes the world seem less hostile and cruel to Jane.
2: The imagery of life and death shows the difference between winter and spring.	'the forest … showed only ranks of skeletons' 'woodland plants sprang up profusely'	Spring symbolises the new life of liberty and pleasure that Jane is allowed to lead.
3: Jane enjoys the growing beauty around her.	'a great pleasure, an enjoyment'	This enjoyment contrasts with the hardships that Jane suffered previously at Lowood and gives her hope.

Chapter 11 [pp. 20–21]

1 a) warm and welcoming; b) housekeeper; c) ward; d) six miles from Millcote; e) Grace Poole

2 a) She experiences some doubts, fears and uncertainty about being alone in the world. But she also feels a sense of adventure and pride in herself for having taken this independent step.

b) She considers herself to be plain and neat. She feels her misfortune in being 'so little, so pale, and [with] features so irregular and so marked'.

c) He is the owner of Thornfield, though he rarely visits. Mrs Fairfax describes him as generally liked and respected, if 'rather peculiar'.

3

Point/detail	Evidence	Effect or explanation
1: Jane admires the house as she follows Mrs Fairfax.	Charlotte Brontë uses adjectives such as 'grand', 'handsome' and 'venerable'.	This setting makes a strong contrast with the simplicity of Lowood, and the change marks a new phase in Jane's life.
2: The age of the house is emphasised by what Jane sees.	'air of antiquity', 'hundred years old', 'old hangings'	The phrases describing the house suggest that the Rochester family is long established, and this emphasis on the past might hint at long hidden secrets.

3: *The house has an air of gloom associated with death and a hint of horror.*	*'by fingers that for two generations had been coffin-dust'* *'relics … a shrine of memory'* *'shut in … shaded … strange'*	*These Gothic features of the setting affect Jane's mood, increasing the tension and hinting at strange things that might follow.*

Chapters 12–14 [pp. 22–23]

1 *By the start of Chapter 12 Jane has been at Thornfield for* **three** *months. Wanting a change of scene, she walks to the nearby village of* **Hay** *to post a letter. Hearing a horse approaching she thinks of a mythical creature called a* **Gytrash***. The horse slips on* **ice***, and the rider falls, spraining his ankle. Jane helps him and then continues on her way. When Jane returns to Thornfield she discovers that the rider was* **Mr Rochester***.*

2 a) She yearns to know more about the wider world , to meet new people and have new experiences. She expresses the belief that 'women … need exercise for their faculties, and a field for their efforts as much as their brothers do'.

b) The hushed and freezing moonlit scene created by Charlotte Brontë emphasises Jane's isolation. She is reminded of tales of the supernatural when the eerie stillness is broken by the noise of a horse.

c) She suggests that Mr Rochester was the victim of unfairness when his father and brother put him in a 'painful position for the sake of making his fortune'.

3

Point/detail	Evidence	Effect or explanation
1: *Mr Rochester believes that his age and experience entitle him to command Jane, but she wisely disagrees.*	*'your claim to superiority depends on the use you have made of your time and experience.'*	*Jane expresses her independent thoughts which challenge the conventional hierarchy in society.*
2: *Jane likes Mr Rochester because he seems to forget his rights as her employer, and treats her equally.*	*Jane notices: 'you care whether or not a dependent is comfortable in his dependency'.*	*Jane expresses the idea that equality is a matter of human dignity whatever people's social status.*
3: *They speak honestly and informally to each other.*	*Mr Rochester asks if Jane will 'dispense with a great many conventional forms and phrases'. Jane replies:* *'I should never mistake informality for insolence'.*	*Charlotte Brontë suggests that social conventions can get in the way of honest communication between people, and there is a difference between honesty and rudeness.*

Chapters 15–16 [pp. 24–25]

1 a) T; b) F; c) F; d) F; e) T; f) T; g) F

2 a) She is already fond of Adèle, and sympathises with her even more now that she knows she is an orphan.

b) Charlotte Brontë uses verbs such as 'rushed', 'flew' and 'flung' to create an impression of urgency and fast activity. The dialogue that follows uses exclamations and questions to convey emotion and confusion.

c) Blanche contrasts with Jane in almost every way. She is tall and beautiful, accomplished and widely admired.

3

Point/detail	Evidence	Effect or explanation
1: *Jane feels foolish and embarrassed that she thought Mr Rochester admired her.*	*She describes herself as a 'fantastic idiot' and questions herself three times.*	*The rhetorical questions which mockingly use the pronoun 'you' show Jane's ability to consider critically her own behaviour.*
2: *She includes advice about women's experience.*	*'it is madness in all women to let a secret love kindle'*	*This argument shows Jane's awareness of the realities of life and helps her to balance her emotions.*
3: *She severely imposes a punishment on herself to help control her emotions in the future.*	*'Listen, then, Jane Eyre, to your sentence … take out these two pictures and compare them'*	*Her 'sentence' is to create a permanent reminder of her inferiority to Blanche Ingram in terms of status, wealth and appearance to prevent her from being carried away by unrealistic dreams of Mr Rochester.*

Chapters 17–19 [pp. 26–27]

1 a) 2; b) 5; c) 7; d) 3; e) 6; f) 1; g) 4

2 a) They flirt publicly, and Mr Rochester flatters Blanche in conventional ways, but neither of them expresses real feelings.

b) Charlotte Brontë shows that Mr Rochester is concerned about Jane's wellbeing and that he understands her well enough to judge what she is feeling. As he wishes her goodnight, he just stops himself from using a term of endearment that would give away his feelings for her.

c) He is shocked, describing the news as 'a blow'. His 'extreme pallor' suggests that he dreads seeing Mr Mason, and his odd questions about whether Jane will stand by him seem to hint at trouble to come.

3

Point/detail	Evidence	Effect or explanation
1: *Blanche enjoys entertaining others with details of how she tormented her governess and her brother's tutor.*	*'when we had driven her to extremities'* *'I helped you in … persecuting'*	*The verb 'persecuting' reveals a spiteful character who despises her inferiors. She is insensitive to Jane's presence in the room.*
2: *She and her brother boast of publicly shaming the governess and tutor over their relationship and getting them dismissed.*	*'I promise you the public soon had the benefit of our discovery.'*	*Blanche uses a triumphant tone.*
3: *Blanche is rude to her mother in public.*	*She interrupts her mother to stop her from speaking, and her mother meekly accepts it. 'My lily-flower, you are right now, as always.'*	*Blanche shows little respect for others and no sense of duty to her mother. She appears as spoilt as John Reed.*

Chapters 20–22 [pp. 28–29]

1 a) He was attacked by Grace Poole; b) Bessie's husband, Robert; c) Gateshead Hall; d) with forgiveness; e) at a stile

2 a) The setting creates a sense of horror: a dim, candle-lit room with a silent, bleeding man and the distorted images of Christ and his apostles. Jane is troubled by thoughts of what or who had attacked Mr Mason and the secrets hidden beyond the locked door.

b) When Jane's uncle, John Eyre, wrote to Mrs Reed that he wanted to adopt Jane and make her his heir, Mrs Reed told him that Jane had died at Lowood School.

c) They have no kind feelings for one another or for anybody else. Eliza has strong religious beliefs but is a bitter character, and Georgiana is idle and empty-headed.

3

Point/detail	Evidence	Effect or explanation
1: The weather is conveyed through vivid detail.	The colours are attractive: 'blue' and 'golden redness', and the clouds are not threatening.	The weather acts as a metaphor for Jane's mood – 'I felt glad' – as she returns to Mr Rochester.
2: Charlotte Brontë reminds the reader that the story is being told by the older Jane looking back on her life.	Jane reflects on her youthful feelings: 'what is so headstrong as youth?'	The questions put distance between youth and experience to indicate that Jane still has a lot to learn at this point in her story.
3: As Jane approaches Thornfield and sees Mr Rochester, there is a shift to the present tense.	'They are … I arrive … I want … I see … he is'	The change in tense intensifies our impression of Jane's feelings by making the event seem more immediate.

Chapter 23 [pp. 30–31]

1 On a beautiful **midsummer** evening Jane decides to walk in the **orchard** where she meets Mr Rochester. He talks about finding her another position as a governess in **Ireland**, and Jane is forced to admit that the prospect of leaving him seems like **death**. Mr Rochester denies that he will marry **Blanche Ingram**, and proposes to Jane. As she accepts his proposal, the weather becomes **stormy**. Later, the tree under which they stood is struck by **lightning**.

2 a) Charlotte Brontë describes the weather as 'splendid' and 'radiant', using the image of migrating exotic birds to compare it to the weather of Italy. She uses colours and sensual appeal to create a vivid picture of a beautiful evening.

b) His choice of names is humorous: 'O'Gall' and 'Bitternut Lodge' have connotations of discomfort and unhappiness. Jane is so overwrought that she doesn't realise he is playing with her.

c) The sudden onset of a storm follows Mr Rochester's defiance of man's opinion, almost as a warning, and metaphorically casts a shadow over their happiness. Verbs of pain and suffering – 'groaned' and 'writhed' – and the splitting of the tree foreshadow their separation.

3

Point/detail	Evidence	Effect or explanation
1: Jane regards herself as Rochester's equal, and even morally superior to him.	'equal – as we are' 'I would scorn such a union: therefore I am better than you'	Jane believes that people should be judged by the fundamental qualities of their souls and principles rather than by their social status, gender, age or wealth.
2: She is brave and confident in expressing her feelings.	She challenges Mr Rochester, setting aside 'the medium of custom'.	As we have seen before, Charlotte Brontë presents Jane as a strong character with an 'independent will'.
3: Jane's speech has rhetorical impact.	She asks questions, uses imagery – 'an automaton', 'no net ensnares me' – and expresses emotion with exclamations.	Charlotte Brontë makes Jane's case convincingly, both to Rochester and to the reader.

Chapters 24–25 [pp. 32–33]

1 a) T; b) F; c) F; d) T; e) F; f) F; g) T

2 a) He uses the images 'soul made of fire' to describe her integrity and 'silken skein' to express a compliance that is combined with with strength. He says that her influence on him is 'sweeter than I can express'.

b) Mrs Fairfax fears that Jane has been seduced by Rochester, and cannot imagine that such an unequal marriage can work. Charlotte Brontë uses Mrs Fairfax to express conventional views and provide a warning as to what will follow.

c) Charlotte Brontë uses pathetic fallacy in which the dreary weather seems to reflect Jane's melancholy mood and the fears that have developed from her dreams and the mysterious events of the night before.

3

Point/detail	Evidence	Effect or explanation
1: Charlotte Brontë uses light and dark to create the horror of a scene taking place at dead of night.	'only candle-light' 'perhaps it saw dawn approaching'	Darkness traditionally symbolises confusion and the emergence of evil. The figure withdraws when it sees dawn approaching.
2: Jane describes how her fear affected her physically.	'my blood crept cold through my veins' 'I became insensible from terror'	Brontë's exaggeration of Jane's physical responses to emotion is a typically Gothic feature.
3: Mystery surrounds the visitor in spite of Jane's attempts to identify it rationally.	'this was not Sophie, … not Leah … not Mrs Fairfax … not even … Grace Poole'	The horror builds as familiar characters are eliminated to leave only supernatural possibilities.

ANSWERS

Chapters 26–27 [pp. 34–35]

1 a) 7; b) 5; c) 1; d) 3; e) 2; f) 6; g) 4

2 a) Rochester allows Jane only ten minutes for breakfast and orders the servants to have everything ready for 'the moment we return' from church. Jane is 'hurried along' at a fast pace by a 'grimly resolute' Rochester.

b) John Eyre has business connections with Mr Mason who was visiting him in Madeira when Jane's letter (written in Chapter 24) announcing her marriage arrived. He asked Mason to prevent the false marriage because he was too sick to travel and do so himself.

c) Rochester compares Jane's physical frailty to 'a mere reed' which is easily bent or torn from the ground, but he can also see her inner strength which he cannot destroy. The metaphors 'slight prison' and 'cage' refer to her body, and her spirit is the 'savage, beautiful creature' inside.

3

Point/detail	Evidence	Effect or explanation
1: Charlotte Brontë makes Bertha seem like an animal.	'like some strange wild animal' 'it snatched and growled' 'hair wild as a mane'	The simile and the pronoun 'it' dehumanise Bertha. The verbs describing her actions and the noun 'mane' are words that we associate with wild animals.
2: Bertha is shown as big, strong and violent.	'in stature almost equalling her husband' 'virile force'	This takes away Bertha's femininity and makes her a less sympathetic character in contrast with Jane whose appearance is slight and vulnerable.
3: Bertha is cunning and dangerous.	Grace Poole warns Rochester 'Take care' and ''Ware!' 'she almost throttled him, athletic as he was'	Charlotte Brontë's presentation of Bertha is an unsympathetic one, emphasising her unsuitability as Rochester's wife, and perhaps justifying his rejection of her.

Chapters 28–31 [pp. 36–37]

1 a) three days; b) She is too proud; c) St John Rivers; d) They have been excluded from their uncle's will; e) teacher in a village school; f) Rosamund Oliver

2 a) She does not want to be traced by Mr Rochester.

b) She admires their appearance, their characters and their learning. They are kind to her, bringing her back to health and treating her as a member of the family.

c) The Rivers family value learning. When Jane first sees Diana and Mary they are teaching themselves German, and St John set up schools for poor children in the village so that they would have 'a hope of progress'.

3

Point/detail	Evidence	Effect or explanation
1: Jane describes her feelings truthfully, the bad as well as the good.	'Not to deceive myself, I must reply – no'	Yet again, Jane has the courage to face the truth, however uncomfortable it may be.
2: She is resilient and hopeful, proud of the choice she has made.	'a village school-mistress, free and honest'	This again develops the theme of the status of women; Jane emphasises the value of her freedom – something she would have lost as Rochester's mistress in France.
3: Her actions are based on religious principles.	'God directed me to a correct choice'	For Jane the role of God in her journey through life is very important, and she believes God has led her to make the 'correct' moral choice here in rejecting Rochester.

Chapters 32–33 [pp. 38–39]

1 Jane is painting a picture of **Rosamund Oliver** when St John arrives at her cottage. It prompts a conversation in which he admits that he **loves** but will not marry Rosamund. St John notices and tears off a **name** scribbled on Jane's drawing paper. He leaves hurriedly. The next day, St John struggles through a **snowstorm** to visit Jane again and tell her that he knows the truth about her. He reveals that she has inherited **£20,000** from her uncle **John Eyre**, who is also uncle to him and his sisters. Jane is delighted to find she has a **family**, and insists on sharing the inheritance with them.

2 a) She takes pride in her students' progress, and enjoys some pleasant evenings with their families. She feels that she has become 'a favourite in the neighbourhood'.

b) St John believes that self-denial is part of his Christian duty, and going abroad as a missionary is his 'great work'. Rosamund would be unsuited to accompany him so he is willing to forgo any possibility of happiness with her, believing that she is likely to find a husband who will make her happier than he could.

c) Delighted to have found a family of her own, Jane insists on sharing her inheritance fairly with them – another example of the important themes of justice and kindness.

3

Point/detail	Evidence	Effect or explanation
1: St John's attention is dramatically shifted.	Charlotte Brontë refers to the apparently 'blank paper' and his urgent action: 'with a snatch … shot a glance'.	He suddenly stops talking about Rosamund and focuses on an unexplained detail, building a sense of mystery.
2: St John's behaviour is secretive and mysterious	St John's glance at Jane is 'inexpressibly peculiar'. He then stops himself from speaking, and hides the paper in his glove.	The reader may recognise hints that something significant is underway.
3: The chapter ends without explanation, creating a kind of cliff-hanger.	Jane's reaction is to dismiss and soon forget St John's mysterious behaviour.	Jane's certainty that the incident 'could not be of much moment', gives the revelation in Chapter 33 more impact.

Chapters 34–35 [pp. 40–41]

1 a) T; b) F; c) T; d) T; e) F; f) F; g) F

2 a) Although she has no vocation for missionary work, and knows that the Indian climate will harm her health, she reluctantly agrees to consider it. She feels that missionary work might replace the life she lost with Rochester.

b) In keeping with the social conventions of the time, he believes it would not be respectable for a woman of nineteen to accompany a man of thirty unless they were married.

c) When St John is hard and cold when he embraces her, she remembers the warmth of Rochester who made her feel truly loved. Both men have a hold over her until she has the courage to stand up for herself.

3

Point/detail	Evidence	Effect or explanation
1: At first, the scene around Jane is motionless and quiet.	'All the house was still'	The stillness creates an air of expectancy and heightens the sense of the turbulence of Jane's emotions by creating a contrast.
2: Jane's emotions affect her intensely.	'My heart beat fast and thick' 'like an electric shock' 'flesh quivered'	Jane's heightened excitement is like a spiritual experience. In the manner of the Romantic tradition, Charlotte Brontë conveys her emotions through exaggerated physical effects.
3: The pace of the passage changes to reflect what is happening.	Charlotte Brontë uses exclamations and short sentences.	This narrative style reflects the dramatic haste of Jane's reaction.

Chapters 36–38 [pp. 42–43]

1 a) 7; b) 5; c) 2; d) 1; e) 4; f) 3; g) 6

2 a) He risked his own life to save Bertha from the fire, suffering terrible injuries. He repents the things he did wrong and is reconciled with God.

b) Diana and Mary are happily married and St John fulfils his vocation by giving his life to missionary work. Adèle is settled happily in a good school, and Mrs Fairfax receives a generous pension and a home with friends.

c) Rochester accepts the 'Divine justice' in all that happened to him. The final words of the novel reinforce this theme by giving religion the same importance as romantic love.

3

Point/detail	Evidence	Effect or explanation
1: Charlotte Brontë immediately establishes a mood of unhappiness	'sad sky' 'gloomy wood' 'a desolate spot'	Following the innkeeper's account of all that has happened to Rochester, the adjectives 'sad', 'gloomy' and 'desolate' seem to reflect his present mood and situation.
2: Charlotte Brontë uses light and dark to convey Rochester's moods in Chapter 37.	'just ere dark' 'The darkness' 'dusk'	Darkness symbolises both Rochester's blindness, and the darkness of his life without Jane which is about to be lightened by her return.
3: The natural world seems to put barriers in Jane's way.	'all was interwoven … no opening anywhere'	This symbolises the barriers that remain before Jane finally gains the happiness she deserves.

PART THREE: CHARACTERS

Who's who? [p. 45]

1 Name: Jane Eyre
Who: **Heroine and narrator**
Name: **Mr Rochester**
Who: Jane's husband (at the end)
Name: Mrs **Reed**
Who: Jane's aunt and legal guardian
Name: **Helen Burns**
Who: Jane's school friend
Name: Mr Brocklehurst
Who: **Clergyman in charge of Lowood School**
Name: Mrs Fairfax
Who: **Housekeeper at Thornfield Hall**
Name: Blanche Ingram
Who: **A cold, beautiful woman who hopes to marry Mr Rochester**
Name: **Diana** and **Mary** Rivers
Who: Jane's rescuers and cousins

2

Characters at Gateshead Hall	Characters at Lowood School	Characters at Thornfield	Others?
Bessie	Miss Temple	Adèle Varens	St John Rivers
John, Georgiana and Eliza Reed	Miss Scatcherd	Richard Mason	Hannah (housekeeper at Moor House)
Abbot	Miss Miller	Grace Poole	
Mr Lloyd (visits)		Bertha Rochester	Rosamund Oliver
			Innkeeper

Jane Eyre [p. 46]

1 truthful, passionate, affectionate, brave, resilient, artistic, hard-working, imaginative, loyal, principled

2 Examples may include:

a) her decision to seek employment as a governess; her decision to leave Rochester; working as a teacher at Morton

ANSWERS

b) In Chapter 14, Jane tells Rochester 'I don't think, sir, you have a right to command me, merely because you are older than I … your claim to superiority depends on the use you have made of your time and experience.' Her later speech to Rochester (Chapter 23) shows that she believes they are equal in spite of differences in wealth and power.

c) As a child she boldly criticises Mrs Reed for her unfair treatment. She shares her inheritance with her Rivers cousins.

Mr Rochester [p. 47]

1

As a dark and passionate romantic hero	His appearance is rugged and dark, and his life has included travel, adventure and some mystery. His love for Jane is intense, 'I love you as my own flesh' (Ch. 23, p. 294) and later 'he never was a mild man, but he got dangerous after he lost her' (Ch. 36, p. 493).
As a man troubled by his past	He envies Jane her 'peace of mind' and 'clear conscience' (Ch. 14, p. 158), 'hampered, burdened, cursed as I am' (Ch. 14, p. 160). Jane believes his faults had their source 'in some cruel cross of fate' (Ch. 15, p. 172).
As courageous and honourable	He risks his life to save Bertha from the fire. He would have looked after Jane even though she refused to marry him.

2 Rochester's intense feelings are expressed in the words 'tenderness and passion' which convey a complex impression of love mixed with danger. In keeping with the Romantic tradition, his emotions are shown in his eyes, where again the simile links him with a dangerous bird of prey. 'Kindled' is a reminder that Charlotte Brontë uses the imagery of fire to present Rochester's passionate and fiery character.

3 a) He is proud and sometimes unkind. He knows he is doing wrong when he selfishly tries to trick Jane into an unlawful marriage.

b) He repents his behaviour, makes peace with God and accepts what he feels to be the punishment that has humbled him. At the end of the novel Charlotte Brontë shows that he is worthy of the love that Jane feels for him.

Bertha Rochester [p. 48]

1 a) T; b) T; c) NEE; d) F; e) T; f) T; g) F

2 a) a plot device; b) Gothic mystery and threat; c) conflict

3 1: Her appearance is large, strong and dark. 2: She has no self-control. 3: She is associated with night and darkness, whereas Jane flourishes in light and air.

St John Rivers [p. 49]

1 a) handsome, Grecian; b) hard; c) death; d) missionary; e) wife; f) great, heaven

2 a) Jane's identity and her history; b) she can accompany him as a missionary; c) austere and inflexible

3 St John: He holds great influence over her and she works hard to please him; He actively helps other people; He puts religious principles before his personal happiness.

Rochester: He loves Jane passionately; He is not conventionally attractive; He is willing to break the law to get what he wants.

Mrs Reed [p. 50]

1 powerful, proud, indulgent, unfair, resentful, wealthy, intimidating, hard, respectable, cruel, deceitful, vindictive

2 a) John Reed is Mrs Reed's son. He is spoilt and indulged as a child and grows up to lead a dissipated life. He kills himself when Mrs Reed finally refuses to give him any more money.

b) Jane is her ward and niece whom she treats badly and disowns by sending her to Lowood School.

c) John Eyre is Jane's uncle who approaches Mrs Reed with the intention of adopting Jane and making her his heir. Mrs Reed lies to him, telling him that Jane is dead so he dies without ever meeting her. He leaves Jane £20,000 in his will.

3

Theme	Evidence of Mrs Reed's connection with it	How this contributes to or develops the theme
Childhood	Her unfair, cruel treatment of Jane makes a lasting impression and shapes Jane's views.	It shows children's vulnerability and the importance of respecting their feelings.
Justice	She unjustly tells Mr Brocklehurst that Jane is a liar. Later she tells John Eyre that Jane is dead to prevent her from becoming wealthy.	Charlotte Brontë makes Mrs Reed suffer for these injustices by dying unhappy and unloved. In contrast, characters who uphold the principles of justice are rewarded.
Christianity	Like Mr Brocklehurst, she sees religion as being about the punishment of sins. She fears God's judgement when she is dying.	Through Mrs Reed, Charlotte Brontë invites criticism of a severe approach to Christian practice which shows no real love towards other people.

Helen Burns [p. 51]

1 a) F; b) T; c) F; d) NEE; e) T; f) T; g) T

2 a) being inattentive and untidy; b) 'full of goodness' (Ch. 6, p. 67); c) erecting a headstone in Brocklebridge churchyard.

3

	Helen's view	Jane's view
Miss Scatcherd	She is severe but her punishments are justified by Helen's faults.	She is cruel, and should be resisted.
Treatment of others	Be good to everyone, no matter what they do to you.	Be good to those who are good to you.
Holding a grudge	Life is too short for animosity.	She will never forget or forgive Mrs Reed and her son.

Miss Temple [p. 52]

1

Statement	Evidence
She is not afraid of Mr Brocklehurst.	*She laughs at his absurdity and disagrees with him in Chapter 7.*
She cares about her students' welfare.	*She orders bread and cheese when the breakfast porridge is burnt.*
She is particularly fond of Helen Burns.	*She treats her affectionately and enjoys conversation with her.*
She is active in seeking justice for Jane.	*She writes to Mr Lloyd to learn the truth and clear Jane's name.*

2

	Miss Temple	Diana Rivers
Appearance	*Tall, fair with refined features*	*'handsome' and 'vigorous'*
Education	*A learned, sensitive superintendent of the school who provides an excellent education*	*Accomplished and well read*
Jane's feelings towards them	*Regards her with awe and gratitude. Values her serene influence.*	*Finds comfort in her care. Admires and enjoys learning from her.*

Mr Brocklehurst, Mrs Fairfax, Grace Poole [p. 53]

1

Quotation	Mr Brocklehurst	Mrs Fairfax	Grace Poole
'a black pillar … straight, narrow, sable-clad shape' (Ch. 4, p. 38)	✓		
'as companionless as a prisoner in his dungeon' (Ch. 17, p. 191)			✓
'My heart really warmed to the worthy lady' (Ch. 11, p. 115)		✓	
'it is not everyone could fill her shoes – not for all the money she gets' (Ch. 17, p. 192)			✓
'a placid tempered, kind-natured woman' (Ch. 12, p. 128)		✓	
'a harsh man; at once pompous and meddling' (Ch. 13, p. 145)	✓		

2 a) While he preaches the benefit of plainness to the girls at Lowood, his wife and daughters are richly dressed.

b) She considers it an unequal match and suspects that Jane has been seduced. She warns Jane to be careful.

c) Grace drinks too much, and occasionally her vigilance is affected.

Diana and Mary Rivers, Blanche Ingram [p. 54]

1

Diana and Mary Rivers	Blanche Ingram
• feel strong affection for family members • discuss books and learning • accept gracefully the loss of an expected inheritance • care for and respect a lowly beggar • admire a woman for her work as a school teacher and governess	• loses interest in a man when it is suggested he has no money • treats governesses and tutors with contempt • treats a parent with disdain • acts loudly and dominates the company

2 a) She is physically different: beautiful, tall and strong, with a loud, brash manner. In contrast, Jane appears more attractive to the reader and to Rochester.

b) Her presence creates tension and suspense; as Jane falls in love with Rochester it appears more and more likely that he will choose to marry Blanche.

c) Blanche asserts her social superiority in an unattractive way, making Jane's views on the theme of equality more compelling.

PART FOUR: THEMES, CONTEXTS AND SETTINGS

Themes [pp. 56–59]

1 Likely answers: religion, journeys, love and marriage, female independence, social status, education, secrets and truths, justice, childhood

Possible answers: families, the supernatural, ambition, power

Less likely answers: envy, hope, greed and selfishness, conflict

2 a) Theme(s): education / Speaker: St John Rivers (Ch. 30, p. 408)
b) Theme(s): social status, love and marriage / Speaker: Mrs Fairfax (Ch. 24, p. 306)

c) Theme(s): female independence / Speaker: Jane (Ch. 12, p. 130)

d) Theme(s): religion / Speaker: Helen Burns (Ch. 9, p. 97)

e) Theme(s): love and marriage / Speaker: Mr Rochester (Ch. 37, p. 513)

f) Theme(s): childhood, secrets and truths, justice / Speaker: Mr Brocklehurst (Ch. 4, p. 41)

3 a) They are confident, well-educated women with strong principles. Jane's admiration and respect for them influences the reader's understanding of their characters.

b) Jane admires their ability to support themselves by working. Although they are not treated as they deserve by their employers, they retain their dignity and self-respect. All of them marry men who deserve them and whom they love, instead of settling for financial security at the expense of happiness.

4 a) Mr Brocklehurst's religious doctrine is harsh, but Charlotte Brontë mocks him by showing his attitude to be false and hypocritical.

b) Helen Burns believes that it is her Christian duty to suffer in this life, and she looks forward to being in heaven after death.

c) St John Rivers is inflexible in his beliefs, putting his austere devotion to duties above mere human happiness.

ANSWERS

5 a) John Reed's spoilt character is reflected in his hatred of school and eventual expulsion.

b) Miss Temple represents enlightened education by giving the girls a serene atmosphere and excellent education.

c) Adèle Varens is used by Charlotte Brontë to show the improving effects of education when she is tutored by Jane.

6 *Charlotte Brontë uses the story to explore ideas about love and marriage through Jane's experiences and observations. The novel suggests that a **happy** marriage is based on **love**. The man and woman should have shared **values** and feel **equal** to each other. Charlotte Brontë uses **Blanche Ingram** to show that marriage in her day was often based on **wealth** and social status rather than real affection. Jane almost agrees to marry **St John Rivers** out of a sense of **duty**, but is stopped from doing so when she hears Rochester's call. Charlotte Brontë implies that Rochester finally **deserves** Jane after repenting his errors and being humbled by **blindness** and the loss of his hand.*

9

Point/detail	Evidence	Effect or explanation
1: *Rochester feels humbled by his physical condition and grateful to Jane.*	*'I am no better than the old lightning-struck chestnut-tree'*	*Rochester's reference to the chestnut-tree shows how he has fallen from a position of pride to one of humility.*
2: *Jane still loves and values him in spite of his condition.*	*Jane uses an extended metaphor to reassure Rochester: 'you are green and vigorous …'.*	*Jane sees Rochester as full of life, and by implication Brontë suggests that their love is too.*
3: *We are reminded of Jane's position on marriage from Chapter 24.*	*She writes to her uncle, John Eyre to seek a 'small … independency' because she dislikes the idea of being wholly kept by her husband.*	*The fortune Jane inherits makes her independent, so her decision to marry Rochester is her choice based on love, not necessity.*

Contexts [pp. 60–61]

1 a) her own experience at Cowan Bridge; **b)** There were few private schools for girls; **c)** little more than a servant; **d)** Gothic; **e)** Mr Brocklehurst, Helen Burns and St John; **f)** Bertha and Blanche Ingram; **g)** Currer Bell

2 a) Brontë suggests that although institutions like Lowood were set up to help the poor, they often did so grudgingly, showing no real compassion. The people in charge could be hypocritical and cruel, while the inmates were powerless.

b) Jane speaks out when she is an impoverished, dependent young girl who would have been expected to be seen and not heard. Later, she challenges St John in a way that would not have been expected of a young woman at the time.

c) Celine was the mistress of Rochester and another man, but her life ended in ruin. Her story may be seen as a warning to young women that men will take advantage if they can – an idea expressed by Mrs Fairfax to Jane (Ch. 24, pp. 305–6).

3

Character	When	What Jane says
Mrs Reed	After Mr Brocklehurst has agreed to Jane going to Lockwood	*That she will never call her aunt again or have anything to do with her, and will tell the world how cruelly she was treated.*
Helen Burns	When Helen has been punished by a teacher	*That, if punished in the same way, she would break the teacher's rod under her nose.*
Mr Rochester	Just before he proposes to her	*That she is his equal in spite of their social differences because she has as much soul and heart as him.*
St John Rivers	When he has asked her to join him in India as his wife	*That she could accompany him on his missionary work as an assistant without being his wife.*

Settings [pp. 62–3]

1 Gateshead Hall: Jane is locked in the red-room. She returns when Mrs Reed is dying.

Lowood School: Jane is humiliated by Mr Brocklehurst but makes friends, and becomes happy and well educated.

Thornfield Hall: Jane meets and falls in love with Mr Rochester and finds out that he is already married. She flees but eventually returns to find Thornfield ruined by fire.

Marsh End: Jane is taken in and looked after by the Rivers family. She becomes a school teacher at Morton. St John proposes.

Ferndean Manor: Jane finds Mr Rochester seriously injured. She accepts his second proposal and lives happily ever after.

2 a) 1: 'one of the largest and stateliest' rooms; 2: 'chill' and 'silent'; 3: 'it was in this chamber he breathed his last'

Comment on the atmosphere: An intimidating room for a small child, especially with its associations with death.

b) 1: 'a fairy place … a pretty drawing room'; 2: 'grand … dark and low'; 3: 'a shrine of memory'

Comment on the atmosphere: Behind its rich, public face are hints of the secret that Thornfield conceals.

c) 1: 'deep buried in a wood'; 2: 'dank and green … decaying walls'; 3: 'quite a desolate spot'

Comment on the atmosphere: Its dark, brooding atmosphere matches Rochester's mood at this stage in the story.

3

	Leaving Thornfield (Ch. 27, pp. 368–70)	Returning to Thornfield (Ch. 36, pp. 487–88)
Jane's mood	Dreary, unaware of her surroundings, delirious with grief	Eager and full of happy anticipation 'My heart leapt up' She also feels natural anxiety about meeting Rochester again.
Imagery she uses to describe herself	Compares herself to someone going to the gallows	'like the messenger-pigeon flying home'
Sense of what will follow	Completely unknown: the coach is destined for an unnamed place 'a long way off'. She was 'shut in' as the vehicle rolled on its way – she is not in control.	Everything is familiar so Jane feels as if she is coming home. 'Your master may be beyond the British channel … who besides him is there …' suggests that all may not be well.

PART FIVE: FORM, STRUCTURE AND LANGUAGE

Form [p. 65]

1 a) prose fiction; b) chronologically; c) Bildungsroman

2 Some of the common features of the Gothic genre such as dark, mysterious stately homes and a sense of looming mystery or danger are central to the novel. Jane Eyre is alone and vulnerable like many of the central female characters in Gothic fiction.

3 a) The weather is seen as a powerful, natural force and as a metaphor for characters' moods or situations. Charlotte Brontë uses pathetic fallacy, for example in making the weather conditions for Rochester's proposal echo and reinforce Jane's happiness.

b) At the start, Jane is afraid of what life with her poor Eyre relations would be like. Her experiences and observations in the course of her story help her to understand and respect poor people such as her students and their families at Morton.

c) Charlotte Brontë gives characters such as Jane and Rochester intense emotions which influence their judgement and sometimes have physical effects.

Structure [pp. 66–67]

1 a) 3; b) 1; c) 4; d) 5; e) 2

2

	How she travels	How Jane's character is developed
From Gateshead to Lowood School (Chapter 5)	Fifty miles, alone as a young child in the care of the coach driver.	It shows her relief at leaving Gateshead and excitement at the prospect of going to school.
From Thornfield to Marsh End (Chapter 28)	By coach and on foot with no money. Into the unknown.	Her desperate state elicits our sympathy. She shows courage and independence by breaking all her links with Thornfield.

3 a) years (Ch. 2, p. 19); b) memorable (Ch. 8, p. 87);
c) headstrong (Ch. 22, p. 281); d) then (Ch. 27, p. 370);
e) review (Ch. 28, p. 378); f) narrative (Ch. 38, p. 519)

4

Point/detail	Evidence	Effect or explanation
1: The narrator points out the significance of this journey.	She uses the metaphors of a 'new chapter' and a 'new scene in a play'.	Charlotte Brontë consciously shows that the narrator is shaping her 'autobiography' and creating a sense of anticipation of what will follow.
2: Brontë describes Jane's feelings as a mixture of anxiety, fear and excitement.	'not very tranquil in my mind' 'quite alone in the world' 'The charm of adventure' 'the glow of pride'	Intense, mixed feelings emphasise the significance of the shift to a new phase in Jane's life. Although her mind is not 'tranquil', and she appears vulnerable, 'alone in the world', the words 'pride', 'charm' and 'adventure' convey the idea that she is excited. This description makes the reader sympathetic and curious about what happens next.
3: The weather helps to build tension.	'the night misty'	The mist might be seen as a metaphor for Jane's inability to see what she is heading towards at Thornfield.

Language [pp. 68–70]

1 a) F; b) T; c) F; d) T; e) T; f) F; g) F

2 a) The extended metaphor of barren ground symbolises Blanche's fixed attitudes, and shows her inability to develop her mind and character, in strong contrast to Jane. Blanche's lack of independent thought and feelings is expressed in the idea that 'nothing bloomed spontaneously' to bring 'freshness'.

b) By associating St John with freezing cold, Charlotte Brontë suggests that he is devoid of the warm emotions that Jane values in Rochester.

c) Jane's intensely passionate nature is symbolised by the heat of fire. Her strength of character is compared with silk, a thread which has great strength in spite of its soft and pliable qualities.

d) Rochester shares Jane's fiery, passionate nature and she feels warmed by his presence. This contrasts with the chilling effect that St John Rivers has on her.

3

	Examples of Gothic imagery	Effect or explanation
Jane's thoughts in the red-room (Ch. 2, p. 20–21)	'a dimly gleaming mirror' 'dead men … revisiting the earth' A sudden mysterious light Jane's physical sensations of horror	Charlotte Brontë builds tension through Jane's fears and imaginings in the dark, gloomy room. Her intense expression of emotion makes her appear all the more vulnerable.
The night of the fire in Rochester's room (Ch. 15, p. 173)	Middle of the night 'marrow-freezing' 'demoniac laugh'	The effect is dramatic as Charlotte Brontë starts by using soft, mysterious sounds to create an understated sense of horror which builds, with the laugh, to a moment of real danger.

ANSWERS

Thornfield Hall on Jane's return (Ch. 36, pp. 489–90)	'blackened ruin' 'the silence of death' 'grim blackness' and mystery about what has happened	This is the classic Gothic setting of a ruined stately home. Its references to death and destruction build suspense about whether Jane will find Rochester alive.

4

Point/detail	Evidence	Effect or explanation
1: Charlotte Brontë uses personification to present the natural world.	'a kindly star' 'the moon shut herself wholly within her chamber'	This reflects the Romantic fallacy that nature can feel human emotions. It makes Charlotte Brontë's description more vivid.
2: Nature seems to share or react to characters' emotions.	'the calmness of the air and sky forbade apprehensions'	This intensifies the reader's understanding of characters' feelings.
3: Charlotte Brontë describes nature at significant moments in the story.	On the night of Rochester's proposal, lightning strikes the chestnut tree.	Charlotte Brontë uses nature to make significant moments more memorable, or to convey a mood of foreboding or anticipation.

PART SIX: PROGRESS BOOSTER

Expressing and explaining ideas [pp. 72–3]

2 Student A: Mid

Clear point that provides evidence in the form of a quotation; explanation is not developed; no sense of the author at work.

Student B: High

Clear point with integrated quotation; reference both to the author and to the reader's response; more textual detail; interpretative comments and links to another character (i.e. Jane).

3 The word 'vanquishing' suggests that Blanche likes to establish her own superiority over the governess, almost as if it is a power struggle between them.

4, 5 and 6

Possible answer: Charlotte Brontë **implies** that Blanche is not suited to Rochester when Jane **reveals** she 'could not charm him'. It not only **suggests** there is little attraction between the two in spite of Blanche's efforts, but also **indicates** that Jane is astute enough to understand better than Blanche what is going on.

Making inferences and interpretations [p. 74]

1 Simple point: first sentence; develops: second sentence; inference: third sentence

2 b)

Writing about context [p. 75]

1 b)

2 c)

Structure and linking of paragraphs [pp. 76–7]

1 Topic sentence: *Charlotte Brontë presents Jane as someone who makes her own judgements.*

Quotation word: *'forbearance'*

Explains: *The word 'forbearance' reflects Helen's Christian principles of acceptance.*

3 Topic sentence: *Charlotte Brontë presents Diana as a strong, independent woman who is a role model for Jane.*

Short sentence and change in ideas: *At the end of the novel Charlotte Brontë rewards Diana's goodness.*

Links: *who, even though, and, implying, like Jane*

Writing skills [p. 78–9]

3 **Brontë** uses **journeys** as **structural devices** marking the shifts between stages of Jane's life. Her **experience** of travel reflects Jane's emotions; for example, her **loneliness** is **symbolised** by the empty coach that drives her away from **Thornfield**. The 'place a long way off' is a **metaphor** which **implies** that her future is uncertain.

4 When Charlotte Brontë gives the Lowood superintendent the name of 'Temple', we think of holy places, which are associated with goodness and spiritual growth. This is an apt choice because Miss Temple is a person 'full of goodness' who has strong principles. She sets an excellent example to the girls in her care.

5 Student B

6 Mrs Fairfax <u>tries</u> to make Jane see that she <u>is</u> at risk of being seduced by Rochester and <u>wants</u> to put Jane on her guard. She <u>warns</u> Jane that 'all is not gold that glitters'. This proverb <u>is</u> an image Charlotte Brontë <u>uses</u> to imply that Jane <u>is</u> tempted by Rochester's wealth.

Tackling exam tasks [pp. 80–1]

1 <u>Explain</u> how <u>Charlotte Brontë</u> <u>explores ideas</u> about <u>social status</u> in the novel.

Write about:

- <u>Ideas</u> about <u>status and wealth</u> in <u>society</u>
- How <u>Charlotte Brontë</u> <u>presents</u> those ideas

Sample answers (pp. 82–4)

1 Student A: Expert viewpoint 1

Student B: Expert viewpoint 2

3 Student A: Expert viewpoint 2

Student B: Expert viewpoint 1